LOVING VINCENT

A MAFIA ROMANCE NOVELLA

NIKITA SLATER

ONE

"Are you fucking kidding me?" Vince snarled.

He stood slowly from behind his desk and shot Jared the type of glare he reserved for people that knew they truly screwed up. Usually the life expectancy that followed was extremely short. Of course, he wasn't going to off his business partner and best friend just because his plan wasn't going smoothly, but he was going to make the other man deeply uncomfortable for a few minutes.

Cracking his tattooed, scarred hands he placed his knuckles on the top of his desk, which was littered with papers, and growled, "How exactly did things not go according to your plan? You told me to trust you with this. That you would make sure Enrico would get the information he needed to make the hit. Now you're telling me it won't go down as planned? Am I getting this right?"

Jared nodded his big, shaggy head and looked grim. "That about sums it up. There were unforeseen circumstances."

Vince breathed in through his nose, trying to call up some patience, a quality he wasn't known for. "Tell me."

"The girl refuses to cooperate."

He frowned, trying to recall a girl. He hadn't actually been briefed on many of the details. It hadn't been necessary. That's what he had people for. He just needed the hit done, so the fucker that cut off one of Vince's suppliers was taken out and used as a message for anyone else that thought prison was a safe haven from his wrath.

"What girl?" he asked impatiently.

"The health nurse that oversees Enrico's insulin shots," Jared explained. "We're using her to get a message to him. Enrico's gang-affiliated, same as the rest of us. The prison locks them down tighter than a nun's ass. No visitors, no calls. She's the only one he sees regularly."

Vince nodded absently. He knew how the prison dealt with gang; he'd had the displeasure of experiencing their local penal system himself. It'd been a risky move putting any of them back in the pen for that reason. It had been Enrico's idea to go in because he had a minor outstanding warrant, meaning he wouldn't be in the prison long. And Enrico's need for health care gave Vince a way to send messages. Except apparently their nurse wasn't bribable.

"How much did you offer her?" Vince asked. Fuck, anyone could be bought. Jared hadn't gone high enough.

"I ended around five hundred large, just because she was pissing me off."

"Jesus fuck," Vince exploded. "Half a million! Who the fuck does this bitch think she is? A trust fund baby?"

Jared smiled grimly. "That's just it, she lives like a damn beggar in a shack in the old army barracks on the edge of town. Place should be condemned."

"I assume you went to plan B when bribery didn't work?"

Jared didn't say anything, refusing to make eye contact.

Vince swore the giant enforcer would've rubbed the toe of his booted foot on the carpet if he thought he could get away with it. What the fuck?

"You didn't force her compliance? Rough her up a little?" Vince assumed.

"Not exactly."

Vince rubbed a hand over his face, flexing his tattooed fingers over his eyes. "Why exactly am I paying you?"

"I couldn't do it, man. As soon I threatened her, she begged me not to hurt her. She said she has a little girl. You know how I feel about kids!"

It was almost laughable that Jared, who was the size of a bear, could be brought to his knees by small children and mothers. Both men were ex-bikers. After decimating their own club for betraying them by setting them up after a drug pick up went wrong, they'd moved onto greener pastures and created their own opportunities. They both still looked the part with large, ruthless physiques, tattoos and take-no-prisoner attitudes. Most of the guys on Vince's payroll fell into a similar category. Except for the Accountant. That guy was beyond fucked up.

"Okay, fine. Where's the kid? Just threaten the little urchin. You don't have to mean it, just shake mom up a little, get her compliance. I don't care what you do, just do your fucking job."

"Apparently Lola's dad has custody. Jenna lost the custody battle because he has shit tons of money and lied about her mental health in court. He even made it so she only gets supervised visits so she has to see him four times a month, the fucker," Jared growled popping his knuckles.

Vince raised his eyebrows. "Did you have a nice cozy tea and chat with our little nurse who you're supposed to be turning into an informant? Jesus man. So why didn't you mess her up after you found out the kid wasn't around?"

Jared stared at him in disgust, like he had no heart, which was probably true. "She's still a mom," he said, like that explained everything.

Vince slammed his fist on the desk. "I own this fucking city and one little nurse thinks she can fuck up my plan? If we don't get Enrico the time and place for the hit we're going to miss our opportunity to send the fucking Ghosts a message," Vince said, an unholy light gleaming in his eyes. "I assume you have a file on her, with her complete schedule?"

Jared handed it over without another word. There would be no arguing with Vince, even if Jared liked the health nurse. There's no way she'd be getting her daughter back now, she was about to become collateral damage in a war she didn't even know about.

Vince flipped the file open and stopped cold, dark eyes on the contents. He picked up the picture in his long fingers and held it up taking in her sweet, pretty features and shoulder length red hair. Lifting his other hand he pointed at her, marking her with a finger tattooed with the word 'hell'.

TWO

"Fuck. My. Life," Jenna sighed, glaring down at her keys. Should she pick them up, or leave them and just sleep on her doorstep? It was about as comfortable as sleeping in her tiny bed in her tiny house.

Finally, she bent over, swept the keys up and tried fitting them in the lock again, this time more successfully. She shouldn't have bothered though, it was unlocked. Apparently she forgot to lock the door when she left that morning for her shift at the prison. She wasn't surprised, she'd been distracted lately between fighting for custody of her daughter and picking up extra shifts at the prison.

It'd been an extremely long day too. Deborah had called in sick, so Jenna's shift had gone from eight hours to fourteen. Not that she minded, she could use the overtime. Especially since she poured every cent into her custody battle with her ex-husband, Zach.

The house was dark. She reached out to turn on a light, but nothing happened when she flicked the switch. She sighed heavily. She'd have to find a flashlight, make her way down to the breaker box and try to figure out why light wasn't happening. Jenna liked to think of herself as an emancipated woman, but it was times like this, when faced with a spidery basement in a hovel of a house that she wished for a roommate.

Jenna dropped her lunch bag and purse on the living room chair and shrugged off her sweater. She was still wearing her nursing scrubs and running shoes when she reached out blindly in the darkness, heading toward her tiny kitchen in the hopes of finding a flashlight. She didn't make it that far. An arm wrapped around her waist from behind and yanked her up and off the ground at the same time as a hand clamped firmly over her mouth and nose.

Jenna screamed into the hand and struggled wildly against the arms that held her. She tried to dig her fingers into the arm around her waist, but it was so thick and strong, she couldn't move him at all. He didn't say anything, just held her tightly as her struggles grew weaker. Tears gathered in her eyes as spots began to dance in the dark in front of her. Did Zack hire someone to kill her? Was he finally done with her presence as a constant thorn in his side?

She knew she was about to pass out from panic and lack of air. Finally she went limp in his hold, hoping he might think she was defeated.

He tilted his head forward. She felt bristles from his chin brush against her cheek and shuddered. A deep, sinister voice spoke quietly in her ear. "I'm going to move my hand. If you scream, I'll be forced to hurt you badly. You understand?"

Jenna wanted to nod, but she was too weak from lack of oxygen. He seemed to understand and took his hand away from her face. She gulped in quick breaths of air, sobbing at the same time, tears rolling down her cheeks. She would have collapsed to the floor if he wasn't holding her so tightly.

She felt like a doll, laying limp in his arms. He was a huge man, similar in size to the one that had been at her house the day before. Jenna was around 5'7", not too tall, not too short. But nowhere near his size, probably coming to just over his shoulder while standing on her own two feet. Though she wasn't tiny, she felt extremely sleight and breakable in his arms.

She caught a glimpse of his hand as he moved it, and through the dim light from the street filtering through her living room window she could see the dark ink of tattoos. Though she couldn't be positive, she was pretty sure he wasn't associated with Zach, but with the guy who had come to her house the day before to menace her.

He gave her time to recover her breath. She was becoming painfully aware that her ass was lifted and nestled against his crotch. She tried shifting away from him but his arm tightened painfully, forcing her ass more fully against him. She gasped and clutched his arm.

"Please!" she whispered desperately.

"You know why I'm here, Jenna?" His voice was a deep purr as it slid over the syllables of her name.

"Yes." She nodded her head.

He growled from behind her and brought his free hand up to grip her hair tightly, dragging her head back into his chest. He dropped his head until his lips brushed against her cheek, then her ear. He stiffened and then pressed his face against her hair and... sniffed her? It was a strange moment, but she got the sense he hadn't meant to do that. He breathed in her scent, lightly at first, and then more deeply, finally burying his nose into the crook of her neck. It was weird. Especially considering she was coming off a fourteen-hour shift. She wasn't exactly smelling like a bed of roses.

Jenna stood up on her tiptoes, on top of his thick boots so her legs wouldn't just dangle above the floor. What should she do? Just stand there and be sniffed? Or beg for her life? She sensed she was being held by one of the deadliest men she'd ever encountered. And that was saying something for a woman that worked in a prison.

Finally he spoke. "Tell me why I'm here, baby."

"You're... you're here about a message for Enrico Garcia."

She shivered against him. His arm tightened in reaction, causing her fingers to skitter over his forearm in fright. The muscle rippled under her fingertips. He widened his stance, slowly lowering her to the floor so she could stand between his legs, which made it even easier to tuck her ass back against his hips. She gasped, feeling the press of a sizeable erection against her.

He chuckled darkly from behind her and pushed the hair back from her ear, running his finger over the delicate shell. She tried to flinch away, but he clamped his hand down on her shoulder, holding her still. "I heard you have a problem delivering my message."

Jenna nodded, knowing she was dealing with a much different man than the other guy that had ridden up on a motorcycle and tried to threaten her, but proceeded to wrap himself around her little finger. This guy wouldn't be manipulated by the damsel in distress routine she'd been practicing for years for the lawyers and the courts in order to get her daughter back. Although to be fair, she'd never anticipated needing it for some scary biker guy.

Without warning, the man holding Jenna shoved her forward into the wall next to the kitchen. She opened her mouth to yell, but snapped it shut on a whimper, remembering his warning to hurt her if she screamed. He landed heavily behind her, crushing her against the wall. He reached down and yanked her arms up, trapping them over her head by holding her wrists in one of his hands. He ground his denim clad cock against her lower back, unable to reach her ass now that she was on her feet. She bit back a whimper of sheer terror. Taking a fistful of her hair, he pulled her head back again.

"That doesn't work for me, babe."

She panted, terrified that he was really going to hurt her now.

"Name a price," he growled in her ear, licking the skin just below.

Jenna shivered, her thoughts scattering as his hot tongue traced a path along her neck. She was terrified of the man holding her, but his tongue was distracting her, making her feel things she'd never felt before. Maybe this is what a panic attack felt like? She was pretty sure she was hyperventilating, which was definitely a symptom of panic.

"No... no price," she gasped, dread filling her chest. She'd gone through this with the other guy. But somehow she didn't think this guy would take it as well as the other one. "I won't be bribed into doing something illegal. I could lose my job!"

He seemed to think about this before speaking. "So, you refuse to be bought?" he drawled, almost conversationally, though she could feel the chill emanating from him. This was a man who wasn't used to people telling him no. "What if the price tag was something you've been trying to purchase for a very long time? What if I can get you your daughter, Lola?"

Jenna went stiff as a board in his arms, her breath catching in her throat. A moment later a whimper of pain emerged before all hell broke loosed. Or as much hell as someone so much smaller was able to unleash on someone his size. She screamed insults, scratched at his hand where it held hers and kicked for all she was worth.

"You piece of shit son-of-a-bitch!" she yelled. "How dare you suggest I drag my beautiful, innocent daughter into whatever fucked up shit you have planned at the prison? I'll claw your eyes out before I let you say her name again. You miserable bastard! How dare you think you can corrupt my feelings for my child!"

He seemed almost stunned by her fury, allowing her to freak out for a brief time, before he shut it down. Probably because the neighbors could hear and might call the cops. He picked her up, spun her around and slammed her back into the wall, dazing her into shutting up. He loomed above her, menacing in the moonlight coming through the window. She could finally see him and it was terrifying. He was probably half a foot taller than her with thick muscles corded across his shoulders and roping down his arms. His hair was dark, maybe black or dark brown and cut severely short. He had a few days growth of stubble as though he couldn't be bothered to shave. Even in the darkness she could see the tattoos snaking up his neck and the teardrop tattoo underneath one eye.

He stared down at her, fury glowing in his dark eyes. He drew back his fist. Jenna flinched and cried out as it crashed through the wall next to her head. Drywall danced in the air around her face making her cough as she breathed it in. He pulled his fist back, placed his hand on the wall next to her head. "You're lucky I don't take out babies or my next plan would be to go after Lola."

She stared up at him with wide terrified eyes, unsure what to say or do. Though she didn't trust him, she clung to his words. He wouldn't hurt Lola; he didn't hurt babies.

His eyes roved over her. He seemed to be deciding something. He brought his hand up to her face. She flinched back, smacking her head into the wall. He ignored her and brushed his fingers down her cheek and over her lips. He stopped on the bottom one, pinching it between his thumb and forefinger, pulling it out slightly and then releasing it. His fingers were so big his thumb nearly took up her entire lip.

"What... what are you doing?' she asked.

"I have to find a way to get that message to my man, Jenna."

She stared at him with wide, blue eyes. She didn't understand until he started to lower his head. "No!" she gasped and tried to lunge away. He grabbed her arm and yanked her into his chest, lifting her up onto her toes while he dropped his head to hers. He held her chin.

"Give me another choice," he said, his breath fanning over her lips as his mouth descended.

"Please don't!"

"I like hearing you beg," he said darkly just before taking her lips in a kiss that told her exactly how he would tame her if she refused to take his message. He forced her mouth to open beneath his and thrust his tongue into the silken recesses, heedless of the hands pushing against his chest.

She tried to push his face away with frantic hands and succeeded in scratching his cheek. Annoyed, he took her hands and forced them down and behind her back, holding them tightly in one hand. He wrapped his arm around her neck and pulled her up onto her toes, reclaiming her lips once more in a brutal kiss. She moaned into his mouth, dominated, distressed and aroused. It had been a long time since she'd been with a man and she was starting to feel the first stirrings of a response for her captor. She was helpless to fight him... or herself.

It felt like the kiss continued forever though it probably only lasted for a few minutes. When he finally released her lips, Jenna was shaking in his arms. Her hands were still twisted behind her back, which thrust her breasts forward into his chest. The posture shouldn't have been provocative in her scrubs, but her generous curves made most of her clothes look a little on the provocative side. His breathing seemed to be more rapid too, as though he was just as affected as she was. He slid a hand to her waist and felt around until his long, thick fingers touched bare skin drawing an alarmed gasp from her.

"Oh god, what are you doing?" she pleaded with him. "Stop it, please!"

He groaned and grinned down at her, flashing white teeth in the darkness. "Baby, you have no idea what it does to me when you beg like that."

"I'm not begging!" she snapped breathlessly and then let out a yell of shock as his hand slid up her bare stomach and cupped her bra covered breast.

He gave her a stern look, reminding her of the no screaming rule.

Jenna moaned and pressed her lips together.

He curved his hand over her breast and hefted it in his hand. He looked down at her in appreciation. "Nice," he said.

"Fuck you," she hissed.

"God, I'm starting to hope so," he answered back in a low voice filled with grim appreciation.

Her head spun. What did that even mean?

Suddenly he his fingers found her nipple and he squeezed, twisting the tender peak, hard, mercilessly. She cried out and tried to arch her body away from him, tears coming to her eyes.

"Sorry, baby," he murmured, almost regretfully. "Needed your attention, since you refuse to play any other kind of ball with me."

He pushed her back against the wall, his hand squeezing her breast tightly. He dropped his head until his eyes were level with hers. "I need you to take Enrico a message. If he doesn't get my message, I will be very angry. You understand?"

She stared up at him mutely.

She could see frustration gathering in his eyes, his thumb flicked over her abused nipple drawing a soft cry from her. She tried to squirm away, but he blocked her. He took her chin in his free hand and forced her face up to his.

"If Enrico doesn't get this message, I will be back for you, Jenna. I will take you and I will make you my slave. The things that I will do to you will make what I did here look like a lover's sweet touch. I will fuck you, Jenna. I will fuck you up, use you up and then throw you out like trash. You are disposable to me, little girl. You need to nod if you understand?" His deep voice was so menacing Jenna thought she might faint from sheer fright.

No such luck. She never had been the fainting type, which is part of the reason she became a nurse.

She jerked her head in a nod, bruising her chin a little against his thumb. He released her and stepped back. Jenna's legs gave out and she sank to the floor, leaning against the wall. She stared up at him with wide, terrified eyes.

"You need to trust that you don't want to see me again."

THREE

Fuck, he wanted to see her again.

And he would. But he needed to give her time to do the job first. If she didn't do it then he legitimately had a reason to pick her up, bring her home and keep her. If she did the job, as he hoped she would, then he was going to pick her up anyway, bring her home and keep her. During the night he and Jared had come up with a plan B that would ensure Steve Buffalo would turn up dead in the yard Saturday at noon. Either way, Saturday night, the woman would belong to him.

He'd never wanted pussy like this before. He should've known when he first looked at that picture of her with the wide blue eyes and flaming red hair that he would want the beautiful nurse. What he hadn't anticipated was the stirring of recognition as soon as he'd entered her home and touched her belongings. Not like he met her before, but like his body recognized her scent on a primitive level.

Like some kind of pervert, he'd pawed through all her shit, touching her threadbare cotton panties like they were something special. He'd never admit it, but he had to fucking stop himself from sniffing them just to know what her fresh laundry smelled like.

He definitely hadn't anticipated the wrenching feeling in his gut and groin the moment he'd laid hands on her curvy little body and taken her scent into his lungs. His eyes had nearly crossed from the effort not to strip her bare and fuck her on the scarred wooden floor of that little shack as she struggled in his arms. Hell, he nearly suffocated her while she wiggled that round little ass all over his crotch, the intense pleasure making him forget he cut off her airway.

His mind screamed, MINE, like some kind of fucking wild animal that knew its mate with an instant recognition.

Vince had never known this feeling before. He had no other female experience of the kind to draw on. He was probably in his late thirties, although he didn't really know since he was an orphan and gang life was all he'd ever known. What he did know was he wanted Jenna Campbell in a permanent sort of way that he didn't feel like looking too closely at just yet. He lay back on his king size bed and thought about his future and the future of his little nurse. His teeth flashed in a grin and he ran a hand over his eyes, willing himself to get up and pull the blinds. It was early morning and light was flooding the room.

He was a dirty fucker. All he could think about was the many things he wanted to do to his naughty nurse when he got his hands on her. Now that he and Jared had a plan B, he hoped she fucked with his original plan. Because he was a sadistic bastard that wanted to punish her in bad and delicious ways.

FOUR

Friday.

Jenna looked up as her next patient sauntered into her office at 7pm sharp with a corrections officer at his side. Her eyes met the hard gaze of Enrico Garcia and her heart stuttered in her chest. She pasted a professional smile on her face and tucked a lock of bright red hair behind her ear. The guard nodded at her and stepped outside the door, giving her and her patient space. Though he was considered gang-affiliated and certain protocols had to be followed, he was in prison on minor charges and thus considered not a high-risk offender.

Jenna's gaze flicked over him as she handed over his blood glucose test. She wondered who on earth thought this man wasn't a risk. He was thickly muscled and tattooed, much like his associates, the two men who had visited her house to get her to pass a message to Enrico. His head was shaved but he had a thick brown beard reaching halfway down his neck. Jenna thought he looked pretty mean, but that was before she met Jared and the guy from last night. The one last night made this guy look like a pussy cat.

"How are you today, Enrico?" she asked him politely.

She was always polite to her patients and did her best to treat them like humans in a place where they were stripped of both pride and dignity. She knew exactly what kind of screwed up system could fuck people over and put men behind bars for petty crimes when more often than not they needed addictions therapy and a solid life plan. Or the system needed a good lecture and an overhaul on poverty and racism. Thus, she usually gave prisoners the benefit of the doubt until she found out otherwise.

She didn't think that was the case with Enrico though. In fact, she felt pretty sure this guy and the other one that had broken into her house probably needed to be put in prison for a very long time. Much longer than Enrico's current two-month sentence.

"Not doing too bad," he answered her question and then handed her the test back. "Blood sugar's good today. Prison food's better than Mc'd's and the other shit I eat on the outs."

Jenna smiled, despite herself, and shook her head as she prepared his usual insulin dose. "You know better than that, Enrico. You should take care of this condition. You only get one body, one life. You need to be your own best friend out there."

His eyes roamed over her features, taking in her earnest blue eyes surrounded by long dark red eyelashes, untouched by makeup. He grunted his acknowledgement and took the needle from her trembling fingers. His gaze flickered down, noticing the slight shake in her hand. She quickly moved her hand away and set about tidying her station while he lifted his sleeveless shirt, revealing even more rippling muscles and showing off a few more of his tattoos.

When he finished, he reached past her to drop his

needle into the sharps container. As he bent, his bearded chin brushed her shoulder causing her to jump a little. She would have stepped away from his big body, but there was a bed next to her, trapping her between him and the bed.

"You have a message for me?" he asked softly.

Her breath caught and she shook harder, rattling the tray she was holding. She forced a confused look on her face and tilted her chin up so she could look him in the eyes.

"Sorry?" she said, lifting an eyebrow in question and attempting to look professionally distant while her fingers continued to clutch the tray as though her life depended on it. Which it did, if Enrico's boss followed through on his threat. And he seemed like the type who did exactly as he said he would.

She was so fucked.

"You got a message for me," he said slowly as if she were dim and just not understanding. It was now a statement instead of a question.

Her gaze turned desperate and she tried to look away from him, but with a quick glance toward the door, he swiftly grabbed hold of her chin and turned her face up to his. "Give me the fucking message," he snarled.

She squeezed her eyes shut and shook her head. He threw her face away from him in disgust. When she opened her eyes again it was to find him large and angry, looming over her as though he planned on beating the message out of her. Though she didn't know how he planned on doing that with a guard just on the other side of the door.

"Lorry, we're done now!" Jenna called, surprised that her voice was stronger than a squeak.

"Baby, you just made a very big mistake," Enrico growled and lifted his hand in the shape of a gun, shooting her with his forefinger. He turned and strode toward the door.

Jenna folded in on herself, leaning her hip against the bed and covering her face with shaking hands. What had she gotten herself into? For the first time in three long years of battling for custody of her daughter she was intensely glad Lola was safe with her father.

FIVE

Saturday morning.

"Our informant just got off duty," Jared relayed to Vince as they walked across the construction site together. Construction was one of Vince's legitimate businesses, creating the opportunity for his offices to remain mobile.

Jared was on the phone with the corrections officer they'd bribed into giving Enrico the message. It'd been a risky move to involve one of the prison guards, something they'd hoped to avoid. In the end they'd had no choice, they had to have a backup. Despite their bullying tactics, the nurse just wasn't coming through for them.

Jared and Vince had poured through their intel on individual guards and found one with a couple of weaknesses. Some serious gambling debts and steep alimony payments. Unable to make ends meet, he'd nearly tripped over himself to accept their bribe.

Jared grunted into the phone, speaking rarely, just listening to their corrections 'friend.' Vince didn't like the man and how easily he'd fallen in line. No loyalty. It meant he may become a loose end that needed trimming.

Later.

For now, they would await word on the prison. His gut clenched in anticipation and fear. Jenna was inside the prison today. She started work right at noon. The thought of her in the prison while shit was going down distracted him, made him uneasy. As the nurse on duty, she'd have to deal with any inmates that were hurt. Vince needed someone to get hurt. Bad. Which meant she'd be called to the scene, a yard full of inmates.

Fuck.

It was the only part of the plan he was having trouble dealing with. But everything had to appear normal. She had to be there, in her usual place. No suspicion could fall on her when Buffalo died. Once business was taken care of and he could collect the woman, he'd never allow her to step foot in that shithole again. How an angel like Jenna Campbell ended up with a job like that was beyond him. She probably needed the money for her custody battle. He figured that was how she ended up in the falling down shack she called a house. She'd sold everything to continue paying lawyers.

Jared ended his call and put his phone in his pocket. They climbed the metal stairs to Vince's trailer and went inside. Dumping their hard hats, they sat on opposite sides of the desk.

"The message was sent," Jared said with some satisfaction.

Vince nodded, his eyes sharp. "The nurse?" he asked.

The look on Jared's face clearly told Vince the other man was hoping he'd forgotten about the red-headed bundle of sexy. As if that would happen. He grunted, shifted in his chair and shrugged. "She failed."

Vince flashed him a grin. "Cheer up, J. We're about to

go to war with the Ghosts. You're the one who's been restless lately, wanting to blow off a little steam. Didn't you tell me last week you've been craving some blood? Here you go, heads on a platter. Enjoy!"

Jared shook his head, his eyes flashing. "You're a sadistic fucker, you know that? I want every last Ghost to die for what they did to us, but I don't want Jenna to get hurt. She was nice to me and she has a daughter."

"Nice? Did you just say the word 'nice'? Jesus fuck, man, you are a pussy whipped motherfucker," Vince guffawed, ignoring Jared as he stood and stomped toward the door. "Don't forget to take your hat with you. I don't need those safety and regulatory fuckers sniffing around my shit."

Jared bent to scoop his hat off the couch by the door before leaving.

"Another thing," Vince drawled.

Jared looked back, jamming an orange safety hat over his thick sandy blond hair and glaring at his best friend.

"I need some extra security on my home. I'll need it in place within the next few hours. Shift some of our more trusted guys around so they're on the house and hire new for the work yards until you can find people you trust."

Jared frowned and nodded. "You need to keep someone in or someone out?" Though they were business associates, they were also friends. He wanted to know if Vince was expecting trouble so they could kill it together, like in the old days.

"Both," Vince said with a grin of anticipation. "I'm going to bring home a new acquisition and we're about to piss off our biker friends. Don't want them thinking they can bring a war to my doorstep."

SIX

Jenna ran for all she was worth, which wasn't fast enough. She really needed to work out more often. The guards on either side of her were barely breathing hard as they made their way toward the yard with sirens blaring in their ears. She'd just hung her purse in a locker and tied her running shoes when the alarm went off. She'd immediately followed protocol, locked herself in the staff room and called down to the main desk to relay her position. They'd called back within two minutes to let her know there was a medical emergency and she was needed in the yard. Thirty seconds later two guards showed up to escort her.

"Gang yard," one of the guards yelled over the earsplitting siren.

She nodded her understanding. Of course there was an injury in the gang yard, they were rarely anywhere else. The prison had struggled in separating gang from non-gang prisoners, so they'd finally cut the yard in half with a high fence. They'd even had to take away the weight benches and weights from the gangs because they were using them as weapons. Jenna ran toward the fence and was waved through by another corrections officer. The prisoners were laying on the ground face-down with their arms over their heads, fingers locked together.

Several guards stood over them with weapons drawn. Jenna slitted her eyes against the pepper spray in the air and covered her mouth and nose. Another guard took her arm and led her toward a man who lay face-up, sprawled on the ground. She kneeled next to him and gave him a quick look over. There were at least five stab wounds to his neck and chest. She checked his pulse. Faint. Erratic, gurgling breath.

One of the wounds was on his neck and gushing blood, probably nicked his carotid artery. She swiftly reached for gloves from her First Aid kit and pulled them on. He had several more stab wounds, though she was fairly certain the one to his neck was going to be what killed him.

"Dammit!" she muttered, grabbing a bandage and pressing it firmly against the neck wound. Each pump of his heart was one more beat toward the end of his life as blood trickled from his body. They were losing him fast.

Fuck. Fuck. Fuck.

She glanced up at the guard at her back. "You know CPR?" she asked, knowing he would. It was a requirement for everyone at the prison.

He nodded.

"You're my second now," she said. "He's circling the drain. I doubt he's going to make it to the ambulance. Someone's bringing out the stretcher and resuscitation mask. We'll meet the ambulance at the front door and hand him off. If we lose him then I'm going to chest pump while you breathe for him with the mask, nice and slow, on my mark. Understand?"

He nodded and relayed the information to the others, then over radio getting the team at the front door ready for them. Using her free hand Jenna awkwardly pulled medical scissors out of her First Aid kit and started cutting away his shirt so she could see the damage. Oh Jesus. She wished she hadn't. Whoever had done this to him knew what they were doing. It was a miracle this man wasn't dead already. Jenna sat back on her heels and stared down at the mess of a chest with despair. Two stab wounds up under the ribs puncturing each lung, two to the stomach and the one in the neck. She was looking at a dead man.

The sound of a breath gurgling out from between his lips one last time coincided with the arrival of the stretcher. "We need to start CPR the second he's on," Jenna yelled up at her new partner. "I'll need two people on either side, lifting him. As soon as he's on, you put your hand over mine on his neck wound, I'll slip mine out, then press down hard. Put the mask over his nose and mouth and make sure it's sealed. Start pumping on my mark."

She looked around at the guards spotting a big guy that she was friendly with. "Dale! Can you lift me on top of him when he's up? I'll put my foot on the bar and you help me over."

The officers moved positions as she instructed, several of them replacing the ones that were guarding the prisoners. The last thing they needed was for a riot to erupt, and violence was usually a good excuse to start one.

In synchronization they hefted the injured inmate onto the stretcher while Dale grasped Jenna by the waist and lifted her until she was straddling the patient. Her hand was replaced on the neck wound.

"Okay go!" she yelled. "Is the ambulance here?"

"Not yet," one of the officers yelled back over the blaring siren. "ETA two minutes out."

She locked her fingers together and placed the heel of

her hand against the bloody chest ignoring the wounds. She looked at the man holding the pump and nodded. "Ready and go," she said, he squeezed the pump slow and steady as he jogged beside the stretcher. "And again."

She began her chest compressions, bracing her knees against the patient's hips and sitting up to give herself more leverage. As they left the yard she looked up. One of the prisoner's had rolled his head to the side and was tracking the stretcher with sharp, deadly eyes. Enrico Garcia was watching her with chilling intensity as she tried to resuscitate the man she knew without a doubt he'd just stabbed five times.

SEVEN

Jenna nearly sobbed with relief when she arrived home to find her door locked and her lights working. She flew through the tiny house grabbing whatever essentials her hysterical mind could think of and throwing them in a bag. She knew he would come for her. She could feel him stalking closer, hear his promise to enslave her echoing through her brain.

Oh god, why hadn't she just done what he'd wanted and given Enrico the message? It'd just been a date and a time. Saturday at noon. The exact time Steve Buffalo had died. An event that had taken place without her cooperation. She knew that she couldn't be complicit in whatever they were planning, just as she knew now, in her heart, that her conscience was clear. Only her damn conscience was going to get her raped and killed.

For a split second she thought about going to the police, of reporting the incident to the prison. She didn't want the burden of knowing who killed Steve Buffalo. But it was her word against theirs and pissing off the big guy from last night even more seemed like a bad idea. Maybe she should have gone to the police when Jared first arrived on her doorstep, but she'd managed the situation and didn't want the hassle of a police report. And then, when her night-time intruder kissed her.... she'd liked it. She'd been confused and hadn't wanted to tell the police exactly how he was threatening her. Besides, she had to think about Lola. If she went to the police now, she could potentially be charged with accessory after the fact for not reporting Enrico the moment he mentioned that note to her. Now it was too late. Buffalo was dead and she was a marked woman.

Fuck, fuck, fuck.

This day was the worst ever! She had lost her patient, despite having worked desperately hard to revive him. He'd died before they'd gotten him out of the gang yard. She was still wearing the same scrubs, splattered in his blood. She didn't want to slow down long enough to change. She could change when she got there. Throwing a few items of clothes into a backpack, she gathered up her bags and ran out to her car.

Zach was going to be extremely pleased to see her on his doorstep. She hated that thought, but she didn't have a choice. She wasn't going to ground unless she had her little girl and she couldn't do that without cozying up to her ex. Zach had wanted her back almost from the moment she left their mansion two years ago and he'd been using Lola as a bargaining chip ever since. She would have to pretend she was in trouble, which really wasn't too much of a stretch. She would pretend that she'd finally seen the light. She would tell him she missed him and she was done living in poverty. She'd throw herself on his mercy and beg his forgiveness, whatever it took to get her inside the house. Then she'd disappear with Lola the moment his back was turned.

It took all of her concentration not to speed during the forty-five-minute drive to Zach's house. Her eyes flitted constantly to the rearview mirror, searching for any suspicious vehicles. It felt like they were all out to get her. She was mentally and physically drained by the time she followed the curving drive around to the front of the house she used to share with her ex-husband

She got out of the car, leaving her bags behind in case he decided to send her packing instead. Wearily she climbed the steps to the front door. She wrapped the edges of her sweater around herself, trying to cover the bloodstains on her scrubs. She rang the bell and stood waiting, shivering in the gathering darkness as evening descended.

The door opened and her ex-husband looked down at her for several silent seconds, his gaze completely inscrutable. Then a satisfied smile split his lips as he greeted her. "Welcome home, darling."

EIGHT

"Your bird's flown."

Vince looked up from where he was shrugging into his leather jacket. He was about to head over to Jenna's house and collect on her debt. Avery Larson, one of his security men, strode into Vince's office. Avery's presence was bad news since he was supposed to be sitting on her house. Vince sent him over the minute Jenna got off work.

"Apparently she left work early and flew the coop before we could get there," he said gruffly. "Sorry boss. This was my bad."

"Not your fault," Vince snapped, not in the mood to soothe his guy's feelings right now. "I should've put someone on the house from the beginning."

Vince wanted to punch something. Of course she'd run. She knew he would be gunning for her. He'd as much as promised he'd come after her if she didn't deliver his message. What she didn't know was his intentions had changed. He wasn't planning on using her up and throwing her away anymore, he was going to keep her.

"GPS on the car?" he grunted, pulling his phone out of his pocket and calling Jared.

"She drives an older model Malibu. No GPS," Avery said quickly.

"Fuck, that woman is a goddam thorn in my ass!" he snarled.

Jared answered his phone. "The nurse, I take it?"

"Who else? She ran from her house. I want men all over this city. Have them check every single one of her contacts. I want constant check-ins. Let me know the second she's found."

Jared grunted his assent and hung up.

He called back two hours later. "She's at her ex's house. He's that shady criminal lawyer, Zachery Morris. Explains why she's been having so much trouble getting that kid back. I have the address. Do you want us to go pick her up?"

Fury exploded in Vince's chest and he was glad that she wasn't there with him. He was cruel on a good day, but in that moment, he knew he would unleash the possessive wrath that had threatened to burst free from the moment he'd seen her picture. She had run into her ex-husband's arms rather than stay and face him. She would soon realize that there was no safe haven for her. That he would be her entire universe from now on and she could choose whether that was heaven or hell.

"I'll do this myself. I want you with me and two more for backup in case Morris has security guys. He should have a pretty good idea who I am. I don't anticipate much trouble retrieving my property."

NINE

Jenna felt sick. She felt like a prostitute and she hadn't even done anything yet. Even though she was sleeping in an entirely different room from Zach, she was still lying in a bed that belonged to him and wearing a silk nightie that he bought for her. Which was creepy as hell considering she hadn't lived in the house for years. He kept all of her things exactly the way she left them. Even her toiletries had remained untouched on her makeup table. And the man accused her of having mental health issues.

She despised having to accept his charity. Charity that was bought with dirty money, given to him by rich clients that needed a smooth-talking lawyer to buy people off. She wished it had been his slimy business dealings that had finally driven her out of his home. No, it had been the mistress he'd taken up with as she'd struggled alone with postpartum depression after Lola's birth. Afraid that people would talk, he hadn't allowed her to seek medical help for her condition. She'd slipped further and further into the darkness of her depression until she'd finally decided to end it by swallowing a package of sleeping pills with a bottle of rum.

As she lay in the bed next to Lola's bassinet slowly allowing the jagged edges of fuzziness in her vision to close in, she had the thought that the only person who would be left to take care of her daughter was an evil conscienceless bastard. And even though at the time Jenna thought she was the worst mother in the world, because depression is a mean bitch that tells you bullshit lies, she was leagues better than Zach. She had rolled off the bed and reached for the phone, fumbling with numb fingers.

The ambulance had arrived minutes later and rushed her to the hospital where her stomach had been pumped. There she had been assessed by medical professionals and given the medical intervention that she needed for post-partum depression. Not even 24 hours after she was released from the hospital, she sought the services of a divorce lawyer. And that was when the long agonizing battle for custody of her daughter began.

Zach never wanted to let her go. He'd been blindsided by the divorce and begged her to come back to him. When that didn't work, he tried bullying her until she threatened him with a restraining order. A man in his position would be incredibly embarrassed by such legal action so he had backed off and trusted in his own clout to win the court over to his side.

She smiled into the bedding and thought about how she would get to see her daughter in the morning. He hadn't let her see Lola tonight because it'd been past her bedtime when Jenna arrived, and he wanted to know what brought his ex-wife back to him looking for sanctuary. She spilled the whole story to him, not bothering to hold anything back. The added strain and emotion helped to convince him that she was being truthful. She decided to use him if she could. He was a criminal lawyer. Even though he was scum, maybe he could help her.

She was certain he wanted her to sleep with him, but he'd restrained himself, showing her to one of the guest rooms instead. She'd cringed when he reappeared with one of her old negligees, a short black silk nightie with criss-crossing straps up both sides showing an indecent amount of thigh and side boob. His help would soon come with a hefty price tag. He never made a secret of his intentions during their court appearances and Lola's supervised visits. He wanted his wife back.

She intended to be long gone before that happened.

Jenna didn't know how long she'd been sleeping when the doorbell woke her up. She blinked sleepily and rolled on to her back rubbing a hand over her eyes and looking toward the window. It was still dark out. Yawning widely, she sat up.

Zach was stumbling in the hall swearing and, if she weren't mistaken, pulling on a pair of pants. It wasn't unusual for him to get nighttime visitors. Crime didn't really run on a timeline and you never knew when someone powerful needed legal advice because his stupid nephew got charged with a DUI or something. Still, Jenna didn't like having a visitor so close to her own arrival.

Sliding out of bed she reached for the barely-there matching silk robe that went with her nightie and crept noiselessly into the hallway. She knew just where to stand in the shadows at the top of the stairs so she could hear the conversation without being seen. Too many shady visitors from the past had taught her to be her vigilant.

"You know who I am?" she heard the words clearly from her vantage point and gasped as recognition crashed over her.

Zach cleared his throat. "Of course, Vincent Corey and Jared Lagos. There's few in our circles that wouldn't know of you."

Jenna watched in shock as Zach stood back to let the two men that had stalked and harassed her into his home. He couldn't know that they were the ones she had told him about. She hadn't known their names. Well, she'd learned Jared's name during their chat, but neither man's full name, so she hadn't been able to identify them. She felt Zack could be more careful about letting people into his home knowing she was in trouble. Vincent, the one that'd come to her home, that had kissed her and forced her to feel things, zeroed in on the staircase as though he could see her. Jenna pressed her spine back against the wall, melting further into the shadows.

"Please come into my office, we can discuss your business more comfortably in there," Zach tried to usher them into his spacious workroom.

"I don't think so," Vincent said coldly, refusing to move. "I prefer to speak right here."

"Alright... of course, ah, what brings you gentleman to my home at this hour?" Zach asked deferentially, clearly trying to understand the situation. He believed they were there for the same reason any other criminal element showed up at his door in the middle of the night.

"You have something that belongs to me," Vincent said with such loathing that a chill slithered down Jenna's spine. She'd made a huge mistake in running to someone from her past. To a place where she could be traced. She should have left the city and just kept going. But she couldn't bring herself to leave Lola behind!

Zach sounded extremely confused. "I'm not sure how that's possible since we just met tonight. I believe you have me mistaken with someone else. Unless you mean - "

"Jenna," Vincent bit out.

"Fuck," Zach said, realizing exactly who she managed to tangle with. He probably knew better than her what she was up against. "You want my wife?"

"Ex-wife," Vincent snarled, his tattooed fingers curling into massive fists. Jared crossed is arms and glared at the lawyer, letting him know exactly how things were about to go down.

Jenna's head spun as she watched the showdown in the lobby of her husband's mansion. She knew realistically that there was going to be one outcome. Despite his obsession with her, Zach would have no choice but to let her go. He had a keen sense of self-preservation that would put his safety above her well-being.

Fuck that. She wasn't going to stand here and meekly listen to them hash out her fate. She was getting the hell out of there and she was taking her daughter with her. Even though she didn't have a clue where she was going or how she would get there, she wasn't leaving Lola to spend one more day with her terrible excuse for a human-being of a father.

Turning swiftly on the stairs, Jenna went tearing toward Lola's room at the end of the hall. Though, at three-years-old, Lola was outgrowing her crib, she wasn't willing to give up her bed quite yet. It appeared as though Zach had taken Jenna's suggestion at their last supervised meeting and lowered the side a foot so the little girl could climb in and out on her own. Lola was sprawled out on her back with all four limbs in completely incongruous directions that any other time would have Jenna bursting with laughter. Instead she rapidly gathered the soft unicorn patterned blanket around the soundly sleeping child and lifted her.

Lola didn't wake as Jenna hurried down the back stairway. She was both pleased and amazed that she was able to make it silently through the dark house with her sleeping child. She hoped Zach hadn't changed the code to the garage and that there was still a set of keys to her old Mercedes in the maintenance shed. If she could actually get out of town that easily she would spend the rest of her life living like Mother Teresa, dedicating her life to making Lola happy. In Mexico. Or Canada. Whichever border was easier to cross unnoticed in a stolen Mercedes.

She shifted Lola's weight onto her shoulder, unlocked the kitchen door and slipped out into the darkness. A heavy hand came down on her shoulder drawing a stifled scream from her. Her eyes flew up into the face of a man she'd never met before but knew to her bones belonged to Vincent Corey. His eyes pierced her in the darkness and then fell to Lola who was still sleeping but beginning to murmur restlessly against Jenna's breast. He lifted a finger to his rugged face in a gesture that she should be quiet. Then he shifted his hand to circle her upper arm and push her back into the house.

He gave her a gentle shove, closed the door behind them and then indicated she should lead the way. He didn't let her go. She understood. He wanted her to go back to the front door where the trio of men were negotiating her surrender. Bowing her shoulders slightly, Jenna nodded. What else could she do? She didn't want Lola to wake up during this unholy mess and become upset.

Vincent's eyes narrowed immediately on Jenna as she

emerged from the back of the house barefoot, wearing a sheer black lace wrap and holding a sleeping bundle. His body tightened subtly and he raised a questioning brow toward his man.

"Caught her leaving out the back door. I'd guess she was heading for the garage," the guy grunted quietly.

Vincent gave his man's hand a pointed look, which he immediately removed from Jenna's arm and then he stepped away from her. Zach stared at her for a moment and then back at Vincent, frustration etching his features. She knew what he was thinking. She had finally been within his grasp, asleep under his roof once more and in need of his help. Now she was being torn from him and he would have to let her go without complaint.

With a heavy sigh, he approached Jenna and reached for Lola. "I'll take her."

Panic filled Jenna. She hadn't even spent time with her daughter. Her arms tightened involuntarily around her baby and her eyes squeezed tightly shut as the unfairness of the situation crashed over her. She felt Zach's hands tug at her and she took a quick step away from him shaking her head.

"Please," she whispered faintly.

Her anguished eyes flew open and met the hard ones of Vincent Corey. She gasped at what she saw there. The blazing fury and possession crashed through her, weakening her knees until Jenna found her legs sinking underneath her, unable to hold her weight. Tears of humiliation welled up in her blue eyes and spilled over as she collapsed, the cold marble floor pressing against her bare legs.

"The child comes to."

All eyes went to Vincent, who stood staring down at Jenna, his expression indecipherable. He wrapped his fingers around her arm and pulled her to her feet, careful not to jostle her baby. His eyes flickered over the sleeping child before returning to her face. Jenna's shocked gaze didn't leave his face. The blood drained from her cheeks and she shook her head frantically, her eyes wild.

"You... you can't have her!" she cried hoarsely, clutching Lola tightly and trying unsuccessfully to step away from him. His fingers tightened on her arm and he pulled her back into his space.

"What the fuck is your problem?" he grunted, shaking her by the arm. "I'm taking you with me and if you don't want to go without her, then she goes with us."

"I remember what you said to me," she hissed up at him, anger seething from her every pore. "You said you'll make me a slave, use me up and throw me away. I'm not going to let you have Lola, you fucker!"

Lola murmured and shifted in Jenna's tight hold. Jenna loosened her arms and kissed the girl's downy head. Once her daughter settled he leaned down, oblivious to the audience witnessing their tension and snarled in her face, "I don't want the kid, Jenna Campbell, I want you. Leave the kid, or bring her along, I don't fucking care, but decide now."

She stared up at him with utter hate and spat, "She comes."

Vincent jerked him head in a nod and turned to his guy. "Go get the kid's stuff."

"You can't take my daughter," Zach protested. "I have custody!"

Vincent turned glacial eyes toward Jenna's ex-husband. "We both know your daughter was a weak excuse to see Jenna once a week. That's not going to happen again. My lawyers will be in touch before the week is out. Trust me, you don't want to fight this."

Vincent turned away from Zach without waiting to hear a reply. Jenna didn't get a chance to see how Zach took Vince's ultimatum because Jared closed in behind her, protecting their backs. She clutched Lola tightly against her chest and followed Vincent.

TEN

How many times could a woman go into shock in one week?
Jenna wondered as she sat between Vince and Jared in a big
black truck. Surreptitiously she reached under Lola's
sleeping form and checked her own pulse. Strong but fast.
Her breathing was too rapid. She was probably having a
panic attack. She couldn't stop thinking about Vince's threat
to make her a slave, use her up and throw her away.

She glanced at him under her eyelashes and caught him
staring at her with a frown on his face. He was sitting on her
right, while Jared was driving the truck. She squeezed her
eyes shut. Her poor brain wouldn't stop trying to decipher
the word slave. He meant housecleaner, right? He was going
to make her clean his floors and toilets and wash his clothes
until she was all used up?

*Of course that's what he means, Jenna. Because he kisses
all of his housecleaners. God, I'm an idiot.*

"Why's she blonde?" Vince interrupted her thoughts.

She looked at him sharply.

He reached over and flicked the blanket off Lola's forehead, indicating her full head of blonde curls with a raised eyebrow.

"Your hair is fire engine red, the ex has brown hair. She looks like you other than the hair. You cheat on that asshole or something?" he asked gruffly.

Jenna's jaw dropped and she shoved his hand away from Lola's head, pulling the blanket protectively back over her sleeping daughter's head. She glared at him like she wished he would drop dead pretty instantaneously.

No such luck.

"Fuck man," Jared snapped quietly so as not to wake Lola. "You're such an asshole. You can't ask a woman shit like that."

Vince ignored his business partner and raised a brow at Jenna. "Asked you a question. I want to know what kind of woman I'm taking home."

Jenna pressed her lips together in fury and swiveled her head around to look at him with eyes that glowed cobalt fireballs. "Oh yeah," she snapped. "I was so bored when Zach was in court that I had an endless stream of blonde pool boys parading through my bed!"

He sat up straight and gripped her chin hard, pulling her face toward his. She cried out softly, but he didn't let go. He stared her down until she knew she had to give him what he was looking for or suffer more of his dominant wrath. Out of the corner of her eye she could see Jared's fingers tighten on the steering wheel.

"It runs in my family," she whispered, dropping her eyes from the intensity of his. "When I was a child my hair went from blonde to strawberry blonde to red."

He released her chin and let her settle back into her seat. "Was that so hard?" he grunted.

She glared out at the passing streetlights. Was it so hard for him to act civilized?

She didn't know how long they drove, but sooner than she hoped for they were pulling up to a house. It looked like a normal house, not like Zach's ridiculously huge mansion. It was cottage-style, with shutters and a garden. It was pretty.

It couldn't belong to her captor.

"Is this your house?" she asked incredulously, when they exited the vehicle.

"Yes."

He wrapped a hand around her arm and pulled her up the walk toward the house. Over his shoulder he spoke to Jared. "Make sure the security is tight. They are to be extra vigilant and report any activity. I'll expect you in the morning, you'll be on babysitting duty since you like her and the kid so much."

"Fuck, man," Jared grumbled.

"I'm right here," Jenna reminded them. "I can hear you."

They both ignored her. Vince punched in a code to the box next to the door and then turned the handle. He pushed her through and turned to say goodnight to his friend. "Be here by 10."

Closing the door, he turned to her.

Jenna backed away, hefting Lola against her. She was beginning to feel the weight of her daughter in her aching arms. Vince narrowed his eyes to where she was clutching Lola against her.

"Give her to me," he grunted reaching for Lola.

"No!" Jenna gasped, horrified. She jumped back, tripped over something and started to fall.

"Jesus fuck!" Vince snarled, grabbing hold of her and

hauling her upright. "What the fuck is your problem, woman? Just trying to help you."

"I don't want you touching her," she hissed at him. "You can do whatever you want with me, but you don't touch my daughter."

His eyes glowed with either fury or desire, she wasn't sure which. "I may just take you up on that." He turned and walked away from her, down a dark hallway. "Follow me, I'll show you where you can put the kid."

Jenna glanced longingly at the front door but decided to follow him. He'd said something about security to Jared, which meant there were probably guys out there watching the house. Maybe an alarm system set to go off if she made a run for it.

Vince showed her into what she thought was probably a guest room. It was pretty generic; white walls, queen size bed with a blue blanket on it and a chair in the corner. "The kid can sleep in here."

"Lola," Jenna snapped as she lowered her still slumbering daughter onto the bed. "Her name is Lola. Not kid."

He shrugged, and then crooked a finger at her when she straightened. "Come here."

Jenna's heart pounded with trepidation. She willed her feet to move, to take her over to him. She didn't want to cause a scene that might wake Lola up and frighten her. But her body refused to move, refused to go willingly to the man who had promised her pain if she didn't follow through on his plan.

Vince lost patience and, giving her a dark look, grabbed her wrist and dragged her away from the bed, out the door and down the hall. Jenna stumbled after him, reaching out for the wall so she wouldn't trip as they walked.

He shoved her through a door at the end of the hallway

and closed it behind them. Jenna blinked, blinded when he turned the light on. When she finally could see, he was looking at her with an annoyed, frowning expression. His looks were so harsh that his frown terrified her. The tattoos on his neck and face stood out in stark, vivid detail.

"Did you fuck him?" he demanded.

"Wh-what?" Jenna stammered the word, not understanding what Vince was asking.

"Did you fuck Zack?" he demanded again, waving his hand to her outfit. "You're dressed for fucking."

Jenna gasped and wrapped her arms around herself, drawing the fabric as tightly closed as she could. Of course this move just molded the silky fabric to her curves and drew his sharp gaze.

"No, I didn't," she said as dignified as she could. "And I wouldn't."

Vince grunted, still staring at the outfit like he wanted to kill it. "He give that to you to wear?"

"Yes," she said slowly, backing a step away as he stalked toward her.

"Take it off," he ordered.

Before Jenna could refuse his hands were on her, tearing at the fabric. She slapped at him, but she may as well be trying to fight off a giant for all the effectiveness her struggles had. Within seconds he'd stripped off both the robe and the negligee, leaving her completely naked except for a pair of black lacy panties.

As she watched open-mouthed, he ripped her outfit to shreds, letting the pieces fall to the floor. "You will not wear things from other men."

"I... what?" she could barely comprehend what he was saying to her.

He took the three steps separating them and reached for

her. Jenna jumped away from him and found herself backing into a bed. She glanced down. It was a very big bed covered in a fluffy white duvet and pillows.

Vince took hold of her chin, tilting her face up to his. "You belong to me now, you're my woman. I don't want you near other guys unless I say so, you got me?"

"Uh, no, not really," she said, bewildered. "Are you keeping me as a... a slave, like you said you were going to? What happens to Lola?"

He shook his head. "You aren't listening, Jenna. You're my woman now, not my slave. As for your daughter, you can do whatever you want with her."

Jenna shook her head, trying to wrap her brain around his words. "Your woman? Like a... like a girlfriend?"

"Exactly like a girlfriend," he agreed. "And if all goes well, my wife."

"But we don't even know each other!" she exclaimed. "You can't just decide you want to marry someone after one meeting."

He grinned down at her, a flash of teeth. "Not the meeting, baby, the kiss."

She stared at him, suddenly feeling a melting in her limbs as she remembered the kiss. It had taken hold of her, enthralled her, made her forget what was happening to her in her own house. Had it been the same for him? Had it rocked his world as much as hers? She hadn't realized, thought it was just his way of intimidating her.

As she looked at him his expression changed, the sinister thug dropping away to be replaced by a wondering look. He brought a hand up and rubbed his thumb over her cheek. She blinked and glanced down at his hand. He had a tattoo of the word hell on his finger. It scared her into pushing his hand away and sliding sideways out of his reach.

She couldn't forget who he was, couldn't let him get into her head. He was a kidnapper, a man who had threatened her and sent men after her. She was also pretty sure he was responsible for Steve Buffalo's death. Not directly, Enrico had done that part, but Vince had been the one to order the hit. She couldn't trust him.

"Please," she begged, looking up into his dark eyes. "Let us go."

"Not happening," he growled, his expression hardening again. "Don't ask again."

She felt to her bones that she needed to listen to him when he made statements like that. He was dead serious and every particle in her body screamed that he was dangerous. Attractive and a great kisser too, but still deadly.

"Please, can I go sleep with Lola?" she asked, blinking tears away as she said her daughter's name.

He looked as though he was about to deny her request, but then stopped and thought about it. Finally, he nodded. "Go."

Jenna didn't pause, she ran for the door. She was about to rush out into the hallway when his voice stopped her. "Jenna." She stopped, turned her head to look at him and waited. He strode toward the dresser and pulled a drawer open. "You only get one night."

He threw something at her and she automatically reached out to catch it. She looked down and found a large men's T-shirt in her hands.

"Goodnight," he said, dismissing her.

Jenna ran.

ELEVEN

Jenna woke slowly, savouring the feeling of knowing she'd just had her first good night's sleep in over a year. Without opening her eyes she stretched, her arms sliding against smooth soft sheets. She shoved a hand under her pillow and rolled onto her side, preparing to go back to sleep.

Then she remembered where she fell asleep the night before. In the bed of her captor, Vincent Corey. Well, maybe not his bed exactly, but one belonging to him. And her daughter was there, which is why Jenna slept so well. She was used to lying awake late into the night worrying over her ongoing custody battle with Zach, or stressing about understaffing and bad conditions at the prison. She opened her eyes and sat up, scanning the room for Lola.

When she didn't see her daughter she slid out of the bed, reached for her wrap and hurried out of the room. She wasn't overly worried though. For some reason she felt safe in Vince's home. Though she was angry with him for essentially kidnapping her and her daughter, there was something about him that felt reassuring. Probably because he hadn't pushed the sex thing last night. Between that and allowing her to keep Lola, he'd shown her he had a heart.

Jenna caught the scent of bacon and followed it until she found herself standing in a kitchen. "Hello," she said softly, bewildered at the scene before her.

Lola was sitting on a high stool at the kitchen island, facing a shirtless Vince who was flipping pancakes in one pan while bacon sizzled in another. He was talking while he cooked, speaking in a low voice to Lola, when he heard Jenna speak. He lifted his head, his dark eyes piercing her as they landed on her. His hardened gaze seemed to soften as he scanned her from head to toe. Jenna gripped the doorway as she gazed at all the glory that was Vince's chest. He was his own category of rippling muscles. Big shoulders, arms, pectorals... her gaze slid down to his belly where a neat little trail of hair went right into his low riding sweatpants. He was covered in tattoos on one side of his chest and stomach, and down that arm. The ink was beautiful, the work more artistic than she'd thought.

Lola twisted on her stool and shrieked, "Mommy!" pulling Jenna's attention back to her daughter. Instead of sliding off her seat, she twisted around awkwardly and lifted her arms toward Jenna.

Jenna rushed forward and gathered the little girl against her. When she tried lifting Lola into her arms she realized she was attached to the stool. Jenna carefully set Lola back in her seat and looked down at her. She was strapped to the stool with a belt. Jenna's lips twitched in amusement as she realized Vince had created a makeshift highchair for the little girl.

"Wanted her to be safe," he said gruffly.

Warmth suffused Jenna. This big, bad man had taken steps to ensure Jenna's precious daughter would be safe in his home. To make sure they would both be safe. She felt shy and awkward in the morning light pouring through the kitchen windows, but she also felt safe. Her lips titled in a small smile. "Thank you," she murmured. Turning to Lola, she asked, "When did you get up?"

Vince answered. "Woke up about a half hour ago. I caught her before she could wake you up and brought her out here for some breakfast. Hope that's okay." He poured coffee into a cup that had a picture of a bear on the side that said, 'I don't always kill things, but when I do it's because they were things, and I'm a bear.' He handed her the mug and pointed at a container of cream on the counter.

Was this the same man that'd kidnapped her? This man was almost... sweet. Of course, Jenna knew enough to know that men could act one way and be the complete opposite. She'd fallen in love with Zach before he showed his true colours. She wasn't going to be fooled twice.

"Sure," she said cautiously, pouring cream into her mug.

"Sit," he pointed at the stool next to Lola. "Eat."

He set a plate in front of Jenna, heaping with more pancakes than she could possibly eat. Though she was certainly going to try. She slid onto the stool, set her coffee cup down, and reached out for the fork he was handing her. She shoved a huge piece of pancake into her mouth and groaned loudly, rolling her eyes toward Lola as if to say, 'are these the best pancakes ever, or what?' Lola giggled and Vince chuckled as Jenna fell on her food, eating heartily. She'd been so stressed for so long that her appetite had suffered.

She watched him flip pancakes while she ate her breakfast. Lola chattered away happily as if her life hadn't been completely disrupted. Jenna was a little surprised that the little girl didn't once mention her father. Had Zach left her completely to the care of nannies? A rush of anger and protectiveness hit her bringing tears to her eyes. She didn't lift her gaze so Vince wouldn't see, but he must have felt some of her emotion.

He came around the counter to her side and, placing his arm across her back, he lowered his tall body until he was eye level with Jenna. Taking her chin in a light grip, he pulled her face around to him. "She's all yours, Jenna. he can't take her from you." He spoke in a quiet voice so Lola couldn't hear.

Jenna swallowed and nodded. She wanted to believe in this fairy tale. She wanted to believe that this big good-looking man was rescuing her, instead of kidnapping her, but she couldn't seem to quiet the niggling doubts.

She blinked back the tears and frowned at him. "What happens if you and I don't work out?" she whispered and gestured toward Lola. "Will you send her back?"

His frown, when it came, was a lot more intense and scarier than hers was.

"You and I will be working out, Jenna. Period. No question." When she tried to speak he cut her off by placing his palm over her lips. His hand was so big it covered half her face. "But just to appease your curiosity, no, Lola will always be yours, no matter what happens between us."

Jenna thought about it for a second and nodded, her eyes searching his. He had the most beautiful brown eyes she'd ever seen. They were like crushed velvet with some golden flecks that highlighted their depth.

"And what is happening between us... Vince?" she asked shyly.

"Fucked if I know," he said, and stood, towering over her. Jenna tilted her head back and leaned in her seat so her nose wouldn't accidentally rub on his bare chest. He kissed her forehead, placing his hand over her shoulder. His dark eyes pierced hers. "But whatever it is, kinda feels like forever."

Jenna's mouth fell open as he walked back around the counter and began cleaning the mess he'd made. The man could cook, he cleaned, and he babysat. If he kept this up, then Jenna's heart was going to be in very big trouble.

TWELVE

Jenna was most definitely not in love. Who could possibly love this overbearing, autocratic, pigheaded asshole who was blocking her way? Luckily Lola was playing in another room and not able to hear the fireworks that were about to take place.

Jenna gritted her teeth and repeated the request he had just denied without a second thought. "Vince, I very much appreciate all of your help with Lola, but I need to get back home. I have laundry to do, dishes to wash, a life to get back to. I have to work the night shift tonight! I can't just move in with you."

He crossed his arms over his chest and simply stood staring down at her, literally blocking the front door. She tried not to stare at the way his biceps popped out. Jenna was standing with Lola's bag and she was still wearing her borrowed T-shirt. She was beginning to feel self-conscious running around in so little. Though Vince didn't seem to mind, and it was a little empowering to have his eyes on her all the time they were in the same room together.

"I need to go to work," Jenna said slowly, trying to get

through to him. "I need to make money. Especially now. I have Lola to worry about, I don't want to take her home to that shitty little place where I'm living now."

Vince grunted. "Finally, we agree on something."

"So, you'll let us leave?"

"Nope." He didn't bother elaborating, just continued to stand in her way and look imposing.

Jenna balled her hands into fists and tried hard not to shout. Maybe it was leftover attitude form her days with Zach, but she couldn't stand being told where to go, how to act or who to see. She suspected if things went down the path they seemed to be going with this guy, that she was going to end up in that kind of hell all over again. She didn't need another controlling man in her life.

"You have no right to stop me from working, Vince," she said sharply, shaking her finger at him. "Or to stop me from walking out this door. I'm leaving the second you clear out. You'll have to go to work eventually."

Maybe she shouldn't have announced her plans to leave, but she was getting so frustrated she was ready to bonk him over the head with the nearest lamp and rush out with Lola. She must've finally caught his attention with her last little speech because he dropped his arms from their crossed position and stepped threateningly toward her.

He batted her finger out of the way and kept walking, purposely backing her up until she hit the nearest wall. He placed his hand just over her shoulder and hunched until he was right in her face. "You will not leave here without my permission."

"But that's...!" she was about to say 'barbaric' when there was a loud, brief knock on the front door.

Vince glanced over his shoulder, his body tensing. When Jenna tried to peek past him, he pushed her back until his body was completely covering her. He didn't seem too concerned though, not like he thought there were a bunch of ninjas about to break into his house and take them all out.

Jenna heard the door opening, but couldn't see who came in. She decided from the relaxing of Vince's body that the intruder was a friend. Sure enough, Jared's deep voice filled the room. "Hey man, where're the girls at?"

Vince glanced down at Jenna, rolled his eyes and stepped away from her. She tugged at the hem of her T-shirt and stepped away from the wall. "Hey Jared."

"Hey, red!" he said enthusiastically, grinning at her bare legs.

Vince growled and stepped back in front of her. "I'll need you to take her shopping. New wardrobes for both her and Lola. Anything else they might need. Toys n' shi.... uh stuff."

"Consider it done, boss."

"I have to go to work!" Jenna exclaimed trying to shove past Vince. He grabbed her arm before she could rush away and held her in place.

"Absolutely not!" Vince snapped.

"Too dangerous," Jared growled at the same time.

The two men looked at each other and seemed to have a silent conversation that Jenna was not privy to. Each second that passed was another second for her temper to rise. It reached boiling point when they turned to look at her in unison and Jared said, "Go get changed and get the kid ready, we'll head to the mall in half an hour."

"I don't want to go shopping!" Jenna protested; annoyance clear in her voice.

"Sure you do," Jared countered while Vince gave her a little push and pointed down the hall.

Jenna realized that with these two big men against her she wasn't going to win her argument. At least not when they were watching her. She stomped down the hallway toward the room she shared with Lola. She stood in the door for a minute and watched her daughter. The little girl was sprawled out on the floor on her stomach, still in her pajamas, her legs kicking in the air. She was drawing on a piece of paper with a pen that Vince must've given her. Watching Lola amuse herself with just a pen and paper made Jenna realize that she should probably accept Vince's offer of a shopping trip. Lola needed supplies. Many, many supplies. An evil smirk stretched her lips as she thought of the money she could spend on her daughter. Vince's money.

"Hey chicken," Jenna said brightly and entered the room, shrugging off the remnants of her anger. "What're you drawing?"

She crouched in front of Lola and turned the paper so she could see. It was a drawing of a person, the sex indistinguishable, flipping circles in the air. Jenna guessed that it was probably Vince flipping pancakes at the oven.

"Vinz," Lola announced, "An pantakes."

"It's very good," Jenna announced, and, unable to help herself, lifted Lola into her lap and pressed her against her chest. She dropped her head to inhale the scent of her child; a combination of warm sun and juice. "Let's get dressed now. Jared is going to take us on a shopping trip."

"Who Jar?" Lola asked, then immediately forgot what she was asking as she continued to chatter about everything her brain could come up with. Vince, the house, the bedroom, her pajamas, the colour purple, Vince, and their upcoming shopping trip.

Jenna dressed her daughter in the only outfit she could find in a bag that Vince's guy had packed the night before, a pair of stretchy-waisted jeans over top of Lola's pull-ups and a T-shirt with a unicorn on it. She handed Lola a pair of socks and told her to put them on while she dressed herself. Jenna kept looking at her daughter as she pulled on the sweats that Vince had left on the dresser for her to use. She couldn't quite believe that she had free and unlimited access to her child. It was like a miracle come true!

The custody battle had taken so much out of her, she almost didn't realize just how much until this very moment. She wanted to weep in relief, but still felt some niggling doubt, which created fear in her heart. What if Zach found a way to take Lola back? He was manipulative, charismatic and without integrity. He was also law savvy. He was undoubtedly, at that very moment, trying to find a way of getting Lola back. Because without Lola he had no way of controlling Jenna. And the idea of trusting someone like Vince to help keep them safe felt impossible. What possible benefit would he have in procuring an instant family?

Vince was tough, sexy and scary. All the things that Jenna was not. He could have any woman he wanted at the snap of his fingers. She didn't believe that his interest in her could hold for long. She needed to be ready to take care of herself and her daughter, the way she'd always done. All by herself.

"Are you ready to go yet, chicken?"

Jenna chuckled when she realized Lola was struggling diligently with putting on her sock. Though she wasn't quite succeeding she was trying. Her tongue peeked out of the side of her mouth as she concentrated, and her mop of blond curls fell into her face as she leaned over to see what she was doing.

"Do you need help, baby?" Jenna asked, reaching a hand out for the sock.

" 'es pwease." Lola handed her the sock and stuck her foot out.

When they were dressed they left the room together, Lola's hand tucked in Jenna's. They walked back down the hall toward the front room, following the sound of men's voices.

"Until he's taken care of, we'll have to up security on the house. Don't trust that fucker not to come after the girls."

Jenna's heart beat a little faster as she realized they were discussing Zach, and echoing her exact thoughts. Zach wouldn't just give up with ex-wife and child without a fight.

"Please watch your language," she said briskly rounding the corner. "There's a child in the house now."

They both turned to look at her. She blushed as Vince looked her up and down. She thought when she'd gotten dressed that no one in their right mind would find the giant T-shirt and sweatpants attractive but the warm glow in his eyes told her otherwise. He was looking at her as though he could see exactly what she looked like underneath the clothes.

Jared broke the intense moment by smacking Vince on the back of the head. "Yeah man, watch your language."

Vince growled at him and stood up. "Take them to Redberry mall, keep an eye on anyone that comes near them and don't let them out of your sight." He opened his wallet and handed a card to Jared. "Make sure they get everything they need. Clothes, toys, toiletries, whatever. Don't come back until they have enough to last at least a few weeks."

Jenna bit the inside of her lips so she wouldn't burst out with an exclamation about how she had her own money and didn't need his. The reality of her situation is that she had $50 left in her grocery budget and $200 in savings, which was earmarked for her phone and power bills. She couldn't afford new anything let alone an entire wardrobe. She would have to accept Vince's generosity, since it seemed he wasn't going to be letting her go home any time soon.

"Aren't you coming with us?" Jenna surprised both herself and Vince by asking the question that had been lurking in her mind. Why was he sending her shopping with his best friend, bodyguard, employee type person?

Vince's eyes heated in pleasure at her question and she wished she could snatch it back. "I have to get to the job site, sweetheart. The project needs a firm hand."

"And I'm crap at managing the sub-trades," Jared added. "Vince can get those guys to do what he says the first time he says it."

"Crap!" Lola yelled, tugging happily on Jenna's hand.

Jenna raised an eyebrow at the guys. They both looked a little sheepish as Lola made her earlier point for her.

"Crap isn't a swear word," Jared defended himself.

Vince slapped him on the back of the head. "Don't do it again, we're a kid friendly household now."

Jenna smothered a giggle and knelt next to Lola to help her with her coat and shoes.

As they were leaving, Lola held firmly in Jenna's arms, Vince cupped the back of her neck and bent to place a quick hard kiss on her lips, lingering for just a second, as though breathing her in before backing away. "We'll talk later," he said gruffly.

Jenna resisted the urge to touch her tingling lips as they headed out toward Jared's truck. She couldn't wait for that conversation. She was starting to hope that it would be less words and more action.

THIRTEEN

It took Jenna a solid hour of shopping before she finally got into it. That's how long it took her to just accept the gift Vince was giving her, with whatever strings might be attached. She hemmed and hawed in every store they went into until Jared starting picking things out for her. This was when Jenna decided she needed to give in gracefully, or she'd be wearing something even her 88-year-old grandmother would scoff at.

She giggled as Jared held up a shell pink blouse that looked like it should be on the set of Little House on the Prairie. It was ultra-feminine with lace at the very high collar and wrists. What was even worse than the style was the price tag. $149.99 for an item that should be immediately made into doilies.

"Please tell me you're kidding," Jenna said incredulously as she tried to get her laughter under control. "I can't wear that."

Jared turned it around and looked at it, his lip stuck out in concentration and his brow wrinkled in a frown. "What's wrong with it?"

"Never mind." Jenna took it from him and placed it back on the rack. "Not this store."

She picked up Lola who was messing around underneath a rack of clothes and strode out of the store, Jared close on her heels. He moved quickly in front of them, his head swiveling from side to side. From the moment they stepped foot out of Vince's house, Jared had taken his bodyguard duties extremely seriously. He followed closely and blocked the girls with his body, while constantly scanning every store they went into. When Jenna asked what he was looking for he'd muttered something about crowds and exits.

Jenna wasn't sure what was supposed to attack them in the shopping mall, since Zach wouldn't have a clue where to find her and as far as Jenna knew, she didn't have any other enemies. But she was still grateful for the protection. She'd been on her own for so long she hadn't realized how nice it was to actually feel cared for. The warm glow that started that morning in the kitchen was beginning to grow into hope. An emotion that both exhilarated and frightened Jenna.

She tried to remind herself that she'd only been in Vince's home for less than a day. That he could easily change his mind. That he basically kidnapped her and her daughter, after threatening her if she didn't take part in a murder. She needed a reality check. These were not good people, and she would not be easily swayed by homemade pancakes and shopping trips.

Still, she did need new clothes and Lola needed new everything, so she would accept the money and guard her heart.

"Over there," Jenna pointed at the Neiman Marcus store. It was a higher end shop than she usually frequented. In fact, the entire mall was filled with luxury stores. She hadn't frequented Bravern shopping centre since her marriage. Back when she'd had the money to shop here.

Once inside the shop she inhaled deeply and closed her eyes for a few seconds. Then she looked over at Jared. "Keep an eye on Lola for me." She dove into the racks, pulling clothes off of them as she saw items that caught her eye and handing them to the nearest attendant who bustled off to set up a dressing room for Jenna.

She shopped as though she were spending her ex-husband's money and needed new everything, which she did. She pushed back the feeling that she was prostituting herself by using Vince's credit card. That was her issue. The guy hadn't once said she would have to put out for her food and board. In fact, he'd simply told her she'd have to put out. Period. Because he wanted her.

The thought brought mixed feelings. Happiness that someone found her attractive. Desire, because she wanted him too. Eagerness because she hadn't shared a bed with anyone since Zach. Fear of the unknown.

$5470.36, several bags filled with clothing and a very happy shop attendant later and Jenna was ready to call the shopping expedition done. Lola had everything she would need, since they'd stopped at the kid stores first. She now had a brand-new wardrobe, more toys than any self respecting three-year-old could ever hope for, thanks to Jared's fascination with children's toys, toiletries, shoes, coats and a new bed. Jenna had hesitated over the extravagance of a new bed for Lola, but Jared had pointed out that Jenna's daughter shouldn't be sleeping on a queen-sized mattress in the guest room. That comment hit home to Jenna that both Jared and Vince really did expect Jenna and her daughter to move in. Permanently.

When Jenna insisted that she was done shopping, Jared

shook his head and pulled her and Lola toward the Luis Vuitton store. Jenna balked at the expense of unnecessary items like purses and high heels, but Jared started piling things into her arms.

"Stop! I'll do it myself," she said laughing as he grabbed a ridiculously oversized orange purse with chain buckles and threw it on the pile in Jenna's arms. "You have the worst taste in women's accessories."

"Do not," Jared defended himself.

"Do you have a girlfriend?" Jenna asked pointedly, shoving the purses she had no intention of buying back into the shelves where they belonged.

"Nope."

"Case in point, you scare them off with your terrible taste."

Jared followed closely behind Jenna as she chose two purses and three pairs of shoes. As they left the mall, their packages having already been taken out to the car by a valet, they agreed to find a restaurant and eat lunch before heading back to the house. Jared, who was holding a sleeping Lola in his arms, gently placed her in her brand-new car seat and buckled her in.

After lunch, where an excitedly chattering Lola managed to get macaroni and cheese in her hair, in Jared's hair and all over the table, Jenna asked the question that had been bothering her all morning. "Can we please go back to my house? I need to pick up a few things."

"Nope," Jared said, without bothering to give her an explanation.

Jenna had expected this answer, so she wasn't put off by it. She reached out and touched the back of his hand, hoping that human contact would pass her feelings onto him with more eloquence. "Please, Jared. I don't plan on staying there." She glanced guiltily toward Lola. "It isn't fit for her anyway. Too cold, too many hazards and it's not located in a good part of town." She lifted pleading eyes to his, seizing on the slight softness she sensed as she invoked her daughter. "I need to pick a few things up. Just some sentimental items, like my grandmother's good dishes, some letters, pictures, and a blanket my mom gave me when Lola was born."

He stared at her and then finally nodded. "Okay, we'll go to the house. But you get in and out in five minutes. Vince won't be happy if he finds out I took you there."

"I won't tell him," Jenna assured him quickly.

Jared shrugged negligently. "Doesn't matter. I'll be telling him myself. We don't keep shi... uh... stuff from each other."

"Oh, I'm sorry, I didn't realize," Jenna said, realizing Jared was probably going to get in trouble with Vince for taking her. "We don't have to go."

"Nah." He shrugged, picked a leftover macaroni off Lola's plate and ate it. "You should have your sentimental stuff. Vince won't mind when I explain why we went."

Jenna was grateful for this big guy sitting across from her. He had the appearance of a hardened criminal with his tattoos, his muscles and his perpetual frown. But he was really a big softy. Things would be much easier if he'd decided to claim Jenna, if she'd been even remotely attracted to him. But he hadn't and she wasn't. Her libido was telling her that she wanted his gruffer, scarier boss. Which wasn't particularly convenient, but then, love rarely was.

Jenna quickly pulled that thought back in. She wasn't in love with Vince. That wasn't possible. People didn't fall that quickly.

They left the restaurant and headed toward Jenna's house, on the edge of town, in a neighborhood that hadn't seen paint in many years. Jared picked up Lola, who had fallen asleep again and followed Jenna to the door. She pulled her keys out of her purse and opened the door. Two steps into the place and she realized they shouldn't have come. Someone had already been there. Had gone through every single thing Jenna owned and did his level best to destroy it. Pictures lay on the floor in tiny ripped up pieces. Dishes were smashed all over the kitchen, her grandmother's dishes. And the blanket she'd come for, her precious blanket, her last connection to the parents she'd cut herself off from, was in shreds on the floor.

FOURTEEN

Vince had spent his entire day thinking about Jenna. He'd texted Jared more times than a drunk sorority chick texting an ex-boyfriend. It was embarrassing. But it was what it was. He was falling fast and hard for the woman and for her adorable daughter. He'd never seen himself as a family man. Why would he? The only family he knew was Jared. He didn't know much about women, except how to fuck them. And he sure as shit didn't know anything about kids. The little beasts had never been on his radar. Until now.

But thinking about the happy, giggly, messy child that came with the woman Vince decided to claim filled him with a sense of... warmth. She was a part of Jenna. They would be inseparable now that they were out of Zach's control. And Vince wanted to be part of that inseparable unit.

He left work early, after delegating a few duties he would normally not pass on to anyone with less experience than himself and made his way home. Eager for the sight of his new family, he opened the door and walked in. He frowned as he looked around, his eyes landing on Jared who was dozing on the couch. Ignoring his buddy he stalked down the hall, planning the hell there would be to pay if Jenna had somehow escaped the house and gone to work. Her shift at the prison was due to start in a few hours and he didn't trust her not to try and go, despite his denial. He'd used his connection inside the jail to terminate her position. Even if she managed to make her way to work she would be turned away with a final farewell.

Vince hadn't needed to worry though, as he rounded the doorway into the guest room he immediately caught sight of both mother and daughter. An imaginary punch to the chest stole his breath as his entire focus, his entire being landed on the two people laying side by side on the bed. Jenna was curled on her side, her body curved around Lola's. She was still wearing his T-shirt and sweats, which send a shaft of possessive pride straight through him. As much as he'd love to see her decked out in brand new, high-end clothes, he loved seeing her in his stuff. Her mouth was slightly open in a sexy little gasp, and her head was twisted awkwardly because Lola had somehow reached up in her sleep and twined her fingers in the shiny red curls.

Vince backed out of the room and softly closed the door. He retraced his steps back down the hall toward the living room where Jared was now sitting up and rubbing a hand over his face.

"Hey man," Jared said when he caught sight of Vince. There was no alarm on his face at having been caught unawares. Men surrounded the house and would continue to do so until there was no more risk too Jenna.

"How was shopping?" Vince dropped his body into a comfortable armchair, which creaked under his weight.

"Good," Jared grunted. "They should have enough stuff to last awhile."

"Thanks man."

"We went to her place," Jared said.

"You what?" Vince sat up straighter a deadly tone entering his voice. He specifically did not want Jenna going back to her place. Her ex knew where she lived and she didn't need to be reminded of the poverty she'd been forced to endure over the past few years. But before he could explode at the man he'd entrusted with Jenna's care, Jared interrupted.

"The place was trashed. Zach got there before us. Probably last night, after we left his place. Didn't leave a single thing untouched. The whole place is gone." Vince was about to say that he was glad there was nothing left of her to go back to, but then Jared checked him. "Should've seen her face, man. She was devastated. Tried not to cry, but I could tell she wanted to. She gathered some of the pieces, put them in a little box and left without a word."

"The fucker," Vince snarled. "I'll fucking kill him."

"Language," Jared reminded him.

Vince was about to tell his friend to fuck off, but then remembered that he really should be putting in effort to watch his language. If he planned on having a child in his home, then it was his responsibility to adjust to her needs. Though he may need to invest in a swear jar to keep himself on track. He wondered if swear jars came with a credit card option? He rarely kept change in his wallet.

"Besides, I doubt Jenna'll want you to kill her ex-husband. Seems like the type to think killing is bad."

They looked at each other as that comment sunk in. Jenna wasn't part of their world. The dark underworld where business deals were often steeped in illegal practices and only the toughest survived. She would have to be protected; from them, from their world, from herself.

Because the more time she spent with them the more she would see. The more she would understand. And for some reason Vince cared that she not see or experience more than she already had. He hated that he'd put her in a position to have to experience Buffalo's death, up close and personal. He'd done that to her. Now he vowed, he would never do that to her again.

"You're home," Jenna's voice interrupted them quietly. She looked sleep-mussed and beautiful. A multitude of feelings shot through Vince. Lust was on top, followed closely by guilt, and the powerful need to protect. And then another powerful hit of lust made the decision for him.

"Get out," he growled at Jared pushing himself out of the armchair.

"Sure, boss." There was a hint of amusement as the other man stood and made his way to the door.

Jenna intercepted him with a warm hug and a smile. "Thank you for taking us shopping and out lunch. You were very patient."

Vince thought about growling at them, telling them touching wasn't allowed, but he reminded himself Jared would never betray him and he should be happy his best friend seemed to like his new girlfriend.

Jared grinned at Jenna and opened the door. "Any time."

An awkward silence filled the room as Jenna and Vince stood looking at each other. Then the awkward slowly turned into tension as they realized they were essentially alone. Lola was napping, Jared was gone and they were two adults with a powerful lust for one another. Or at least Vince hoped Jenna felt the way he felt, or things were about to get real awkward again.

"Fuck it," he mumbled and lunged forward, reaching

for her. Fuck, at the rate he was going, he'd fill that swear jar with enough to put Lola through college.

Jenna didn't hesitate, she went into his arms as though it was the most natural thing in the world. At first Vince was shocked, didn't know what to do with the cute, curvy redhead filling his arms. Then instinct took over and he dropped his head to hers, capturing her upturned lips in a kiss that would leave her in no doubt as to exactly what he wanted. Thank the fucking gods, she seemed to want the same thing. She returned his kiss with equal fervor, standing on her toes and touching every part of him she could. A shiver, an actual goddamned shiver ran through him as she raked her nails down his back over top of his shirt, sending a cascade of pleasurable sensations through him. If his dick hadn't been hard as stone a minute ago, it sure as fuck was now.

Without breaking the kiss they stumbled down the hall together, hands touching every part of each other they could reach. She tugged at the buttons on his shirt, first trying to undo them with gentle fingers, then tearing at them like a tigress. Vince shoved her fingers aside impatiently and tore the shirt right down the front. He couldn't remember if it was a favourite. Didn't care. The only thing he wanted draped over him was Jenna.

He shoved his tongue into her mouth, tasting her, drowning in her as he pulled the clothes from her body. They went easily since they belonged to him and were several sizes too big for the petite woman. The clothes were left in a messy pile in the hallway as Vince dragged her into his bedroom, closing the door behind them. He checked himself at the last minute and managed to close the door softly instead of slamming it. He didn't need a three-year-old child cock blocking him. He suspected there would be enough of that in their future.

Jenna tore her lips from Vince's and sucked air into her lungs, her chest heaving with the effort. She looked at him with sparkling lust fogged velvet blue eyes. The prettiest eyes Vince had ever seen. In fact, he couldn't remember ever looking at a woman's eyes before. Or if he had, he hadn't cared enough to retain the knowledge of their colour. Somehow, Jenna was different. He knew without a doubt, that the exact shade of those eyes were now burned in his memory until the end of time. He reached for her, intending to steal more of those incredible drugging kisses from her bee-stung lips.

She held a hand up. "Wait, wait, we need to talk," she said hoarsely.

"No more waiting," Vince growled, grabbing her arm and dragging her back into his embrace.

She allowed him to hold her but held her face to the side so he couldn't kiss her again. Vince wasn't having that. He would find a way to kiss her. He swung her around and shoved her back onto the bed where she fell in an ungraceful heap. He dropped to his knees next to the bed and shoved her legs apart, diving in between, fully intent on kissing her pussy until he'd had his fill of kissing.

"Ahhhh!" Jenna shrieked, pulling her legs back and trying to push his head away at the same time.

Vince slapped the inside of her thigh which caused her to jump, then he dragged her back into position, using his shoulders to force her legs apart. Damn woman was really fighting him on this. He wondered if it was sex in general that she was objecting to, or if she didn't want him to lick her pussy? Well, she'd just have to get used to it because he wasn't about to give up that sweet nectar. He knew once he had a taste there would be no going back. He was going to lick and suck this honeypot until the end of time.

"Vince!" she yelled as he dove in tongue first, taking his first sip.

"Lola," he muttered against her labia.

His reminded that her daughter was sleeping soundly just down the hall from them seemed to sink in and she lowered the volume of her shrieks, moans and protests. "Vince!" she whispered as loudly as possible as he groaned into her pussy, lashing her mercilessly with his tongue. He knew he should slow down, gently grow her orgasm, show her that he could produce a modicum of finesse if needed, but he was drowning in her taste and her scent. She was beautiful and he couldn't get enough.

"Vince," she gasped again. Fuck he loved the sound of his name on her lips especially as she was jerking and moaning wildly underneath him. "Please tell me this isn't payment for all the stuff we bought today."

Vince froze. Her words, her doubt in him, were about the only thing that could make him lift his head from between her legs. She lifted her own head off the bed, meeting his steely gaze with a vulnerable one of her own. He crawled up her body, following her as she tried to crawl backwards away from him. Vince pinned her to the bed, holding her in place, making sure she was in a good position to hear and understand him, while he cleared things up.

"You don't owe me anything. You will never owe me anything. What's happening between us was inevitable from the moment I touched you in that shit shack you used to live in. I knew you were mine then, and I know it even more now. So shut up, relax and enjoy, cause this is happening, sweetheart."

He stared down at her, hoping he hadn't fucked up with

his words. He wasn't a well-spoken guy. He hung out with thugs and blue-collar workers, he knew jack shit about soft words and passionate speeches. And he really didn't want to have to go another 24 hours with blue balls as he tried to find the right words to get the woman of his dreams into his bed if she refused to fuck him now.

Finally, she spoke, putting him out of his misery. "I think that's the sweetest thing anyone's ever said to me." She wrapped her arms around his neck and tugged his head down to hers.

Relief and triumph slashed through him as he kissed her, their lips lingering as they memorized her, as she tasted herself on him. Their hands were everywhere, hers running down his back, up his arms, over his chest. He touched her breasts, filling his hands with her incredible globes, testing their softness, their fullness, the way her nipples peaked as the rough pads of his fingertips grazed them. Perfect. Just like the rest of her, from her tiny feet to her sweet pussy, her tits were a perfect work of art.

He couldn't wait any longer, he needed to be inside her, wanted as much of him touching her as he could get. "Need to fuck you now," he growled against her throat, finding her with his fingers and parting her folds. The wetness that coated his fingers called to him, sent a sizzling need to fill her right through his body, filling his balls with a heavy need.

"Condom?" she asked.

"Don't want anything between us, sweetheart, I'm clean."

"Please," she begged, her voice a feathery whisper against his collarbone. "Until we can get health checks."

He shouldn't care, should just take her the way he longed. A day ago he would have. He would've fucked her without a condom, would've laid down the law, his law. But she asked him sweetly, didn't want to stop. He didn't want to disappoint her, even though he knew it was a waste of time and a condom. They were both clean, he had the records to prove it. But he would give his princess what she wanted until he could get what he wanted, no barrier between them and his baby planted firmly in her womb.

The last thought surprised him and he pondered it as he reached into his nightstand, pulled a condom out and rolled it over his raging dick. A baby? Not once in his life had he considered the idea of a baby. But the idea of Jenna in his home, lush and round with his baby, her little girl growing up under his care, was an image he couldn't shake.

He moved over top of her as she spread her legs, lifting them to wrap around his hips. "It's been awhile," she whispered.

"Me too," he grunted and pushed himself into her welcoming heat, the mantra 'go slow' repeating over and over in his brain. He didn't want to hurt Jenna, didn't want this experience to be over before it started. As he bottomed out, his cock touching every snug part of her pussy it could reach, he gathered her up into his arms and held her. They clung to each other as he began fucking her, slow at first, then with building passion. Her cries filled his ears, driving him on, giving him tunnel vision until all he wanted was to hear her scream as her orgasm took over.

She bit his shoulder, probably in an attempt to stop her shouts from waking up the kid. He wrapped his hand around the back of her head and held her close. Pleasure zinged through his body until he was groaning as loud as her, his entire being focused on this moment. He couldn't stop if he tried, couldn't stop if the house was on fire or if a herd of zebras went running through his bedroom. His life depending on the culmination of their mutual pleasure.

Jenna was the first to reach orgasm, letting loose a muffled scream as her teeth sank deeper into his flesh. That tiny prick of pain, given to him by the only woman who had ever captured his attention, threw him headlong into his own orgasm. Warmth rushed down his spine, into his balls and straight through his engorged cock. He filled the condom to overflowing with all the semen that had been gathering in his balls from the moment he looked at her picture and decided she belonged to him.

"Oh. My. Fuck." Jenna announced, flopping bonelessly beneath him.

Vince pulled out of her and rolled over onto his back, one hand resting possessively on her belly. He grinned at the ceiling, his first real, honest to goodness smile in years. "Yeah," he agreed.

He'd never felt this way before. Not even close. He brought women home sometimes. Fucked them, sent them on their way. This was different. He already felt a powerful craving for the woman he'd fucked seconds before. He wanted to do it again. His cock was already growing semi-hard as he thought of how he'd fuck her next. On her knees, her chest pressed down into the bed. He'd fuck her pussy and play with her ass, get her used to anal play. He suspected she was an innocent when it came to anal.

He was in the process of rolling over on top of her again and capturing her face between his palms, when a voice filtered through the door. "Mommy?"

They both sat up and looked at the door. Or more specifically, the knob that was slowly turning. They scrambled for the blankets, laughing like lunatics as the door swung open.

FIFTEEN

"You will accept Sharon's help and that's final," Vince snapped, giving Jenna a hard stare. "You can't do everything yourself and I don't want you alone here all day."

Jenna stuck her tongue out at him. It had been two weeks since Jenna and Lola moved into Vince's home. Two absolutely perfect weeks that Jenna wanted to hold in her heart forever. The man she'd thought was a thug and a merciless kidnapping asshole had transformed into an amazing boyfriend. His every thought and action seemed to be geared toward Jenna's and Lola's comfort. He bought them gifts almost daily and took them out for play dates in the city. He child proofed his home in a matter of days and set up a brand new bedroom for Lola. If Jenna had any doubts about his ability to commit, either to her or a child that didn't belong to him by blood, he'd managed to smash those doubts.

"First of all," Jenna started, knowing how much Vince hated when she started a conversation that way. "I don't have a job anymore. If you recall, some overbearing man stepped in and terminated my employment, which I'm pretty sure is illegal I'd like to add. So, all I do all day long is cook, clean and take care of my daughter." She went up on her toes and pressed her lips against his. "Thank you for that. I'm very grateful to be in a position to spend this much time with Lola."

"Exactly, you need more time with her. Sharon can help with the - "

Jenna cut him off again with another kiss. Then leaned back and gave him a no-nonsense look. "Second of all, I'm surrounded by your security team all day long, how exactly am I alone? Jared practically lives in our kitchen. He spends more time here than you do."

Vince grunted his annoyance. "That's another thing. If you stopped making delicious food then he might leave on his own. I'd rather not have to order him back to the job site. He's like a stray dog, hanging around to pick up any scraps you might throw his way."

"He's super sweet with Lola," Jenna protested.

"He has a job to do, he needs to get the fuck back to work instead of having tea parties with Lola and her dolls. If anyone should be having tea, it's me."

Jenna snapped her fingers and pointed at the swear jar on the counter, giving him a pointed look. He was the one to set it up, so he could darn well fill it with coins if he was going to have such a potty mouth. He grumbled under his breath, reached into his pocket, pulled a handful of coins out and dropped them into the jar. After only two weeks it was nearly full. Jenna was starting to suspect he actually intended to pay for Lola's college tuition this way. Jared and Vince, along with some of the security guys who occasionally came into the house for food and to do a security sweep, contributed.

After paying into the fund, Vince grabbed Jenna by the

back of her neck, wrapped an arm around her waist and pulled her up onto her toes while bending toward her for a lingering kiss. His breath swept over her just before his lips captured hers. Her knees went weak almost immediately and she was grateful for his solid body. She leaned heavily against him, wrapping her arms around his waist.

"My want tisses too!"

Lola came screeching around the kitchen island and slammed her little body against their legs. They broke apart, Jenna laughing, while Vince bent over to pick the little girl up. He held her tight in his arms and rained kisses all over her face.

"You can have all the kisses you want, brat," Vince told her before setting her back on the floor.

It made Jenna's heart ache in a good way every time she saw them together. They fit like two peas in a pod. Vince made time for Lola every day, asking her questions, buying her puzzles and books and getting down on the floor to play with her. Jenna thought he was putting in the effort for her sake, but the more she saw them together the more she believed he truly loved her daughter. This was the type of relationship she'd always wanted Lola to develop with her father. It was becoming more clear by the day that Zach had rarely interacted with his daughter. Lola never asked about him, while she asked daily when Vince or Jared were coming home. Once Lola asked about a former nanny and a couple of times she asked if she was going back to her old house, but Zach didn't even register for Lola. Which, for Jenna, was both sad and a relief. She would hate to take away someone Lola truly loved.

Vince pointed at Jenna. "Sharon will be here tomorrow morning at 9, I expect you to put her to work."

Jenna bit his finger. When he jerked it out of her mouth

she said, "Fine, I'll be perfectly polite and let her fold laundry. I hate laundry anyway."

"Good," he grunted, dropped another kiss on her lips and left for work.

"SHUT UP, HE DID NOT!" Sharon exclaimed, leaning forward against the island where Jenna was pouring ingredients into a bowl.

"Yes! He broke into my house and tried to terrorize me into doing his dirty work. I nearly had a heart attack, I was so freaked out. He's lucky I didn't call the cops and get him put him in jail right then and there."

"More like you're the lucky one, judging from that sex mussed hair I saw this morning," Sharon teased, making Jenna blush and let out a laugh.

It had been a little over a week since Sharon started working in the house as a part time housekeeper and nanny. She and Jenna had become fast friends and, after a few days and a few glasses of wine, no topic of conversation was off limits between them. Sharon was formerly part of some kind of clubhouse that Vince and Jared had belonged to. Apparently things went bad, the gang tried to betray the two men and Sharon was caught in the middle. She'd gone to Vince with some information about the betrayal, saving his life and making her a target of the club. Jenna wasn't sure of the specifics, wasn't sure she wanted to know, but the club was now gone and Vince ran things in their absence. His protection extended to Sharon, Jared and couple of other former club members who went to his side.

Sharon was an interesting woman. She was covered head to foot in tattoos, only her face escaping the ink. She vaped like only a former chain-smoker could and drank and swore like a sailor. Except when she was around Lola. She became a doting aunt with perfect vocabulary and the instincts of a mama lion. She was a perfect addition to the household and Jenna was glad she let Vince convince her to give Sharon a chance.

They were busy making cookies together and chatting about Jenna and Vince. A popular topic of conversation since the relationship was fairly new and Jenna still had stars in her eyes. The sex was amazing and happened almost every night, often multiple times per night until Jenna begged Vince to let her get some sleep and give her tired girl parts a break.

"Shit, we're out of butter," Sharon said, searching the fridge.

"Hmmm," Jenna leaned across her and peeked in the fridge. "We'll need to get more."

"I'll go." Sharon straightened up. "You need to stay and pull the batch in the oven out when they're done."

Jenna shook her head. "I'll go, I want to get Lola out of the house for a few minutes. Fresh air and all that good stuff. Plus, I have a few other things I want to pick up while I'm out."

"Take the security guys with you," Sharon said in her no-nonsense voice.

For the most part Jenna barely noticed the security guys unless they were in the house. She tried to treat them more like friends and less like people who were responsible for keeping her and Lola safe. It felt weird being with a man who might be a target. She understood the need for security, she just didn't know quite how to deal with them yet. She felt like she was bothering them every time she made a request. She actually paused for a moment and seriously considered letting Sharon go to the store instead so she wouldn't have to ask for an escort. Finally, she decided that it was important to get Lola out of the house and go about her life as normally as she could with a couple of dark-clad sunglass-wearing gentlemen following her around.

She pulled her phone out of her pocket and texted Avery, the head security guy: **Going to the grocery store with Lola.**

Seconds later she received a text back: **Bradshaw and Hanes will accompany you.**

Jenna texted: **I'm taking the Lincoln, they can follow.**

She didn't wait for another message, instead putting her phone away. She knew what was coming next, Avery would try to convince her to let the men drive them, and when she refused he would call Vince, who would call Jenna and demand she go with the security men instead of in her own car. But Jenna wanted some alone time with her daughter, even if it was a short twenty-minute run to the store. As much as she was learning to love and appreciate the newfound supports she was receiving in Vince, Jared, Sharon and the security team, she was almost never alone. She wanted to take a selfish moment and keep Lola all to herself. And drive the beautiful SUV Vince bought for her.

"Be back in a few!" she said to Sharon sailing out of the kitchen and picking Lola up from her spot in the living room, surrounded by a mess of Mega blocks that Vince had bought, insisting his little girl was going to grow up to become an engineer.

She had them bundled up in their outdoor gear in record time and flew into the garage where she buckled Lola into her car seat behind the driver's seat. Climbing into her seat, Jenna adjusted the mirror and chair for her shorter frame. Vince had taken his motorbike to work that morning, leaving the Lincoln for Jenna if she needed it. She hit the garage door opener and backed out onto the street, waving in her mirror as Bradshaw and Hanes pulled up behind her.

Jenna lost her tail somewhere around the third light and sent a quick voice message letting the guys know what store she was going to. They immediately responded, telling her to stay put in the parking lot until they arrived. "So bossy," she said to Lola winking in the rearview at her chattering daughter.

When they arrived, Jenna glanced around, looking for the security guys. When she didn't see them she shrugged and pulled into a spot. There was enough empty spaces on either side for the guys to park next to her. As she climbed out a van pulled into the spot right next to her. She frowned in annoyance and flattened herself against the Lincoln as the guy finished parking.

"There are a million empty spots and you have to park right next to me?" she muttered in annoyance, opening the rear passenger door. She reached for the buckle on Lola's car seat.

The scrape of a shoe on the pavement right behind her caught her attention, and just as she heard the slide of a van door and turned around to look she was grabbed from behind. She was yanked into someone's body, a man she guessed, the one driving the van. She let out a yelp before she was flung around and shoved headfirst into the back of a van.

SIXTEEN

Before she could react and twist around and look at her attacker, her arms were seized, yanked behind her back and tied. She kicked out, her running shoe connecting with something soft. The man cried out in pain and shoved her legs into the van. Jenna could hear Lola's screams and her heart nearly burst out of her chest. Would he go after Lola next? Would he hurt her?

Jenna began screaming as he slammed the door shut. Even though she was closed in, she continued to scream, trying to get someone's attention, as he climbed into the driver's seat and reversed out of the space with enough force to send Jenna rolling across the dirty hard surface of the empty back of the van. She slammed into the side, curling into a ball so her head wouldn't hit anything.

As soon as she was able to roll onto her back she began screaming bloody murder again.

The guy twisted in his seat to look at her and snarled, "Shut the fuck up, Jenna!"

"Zach!" she gasped, staring at him in disbelief.

He didn't respond but turned his attention back to the

road where he sped away from the grocery store taking almost every turn he saw. Jenna figured he was trying to lose her security team. It wouldn't take Jenna's security long to realize what happened and come after them.

"You motherfucking spineless asshole!" Jenna screeched going up onto her knees and crawling forward toward him. "You left our daughter in a parking lot!"

"You'd rather I grabbed her too?" he asked, his voice low and ugly, as though he'd reached the end of his sanity.

"I'd rather you stop being a kidnapping stalker!" she yelled back.

He hit the brakes, stopping fast for a light. Jenna was flung into his seat and then onto her back, knocking the wind out of her and crushing her hands underneath her. She yelped in pain and rolled onto her side. The van started moving again.

"He made me sign custody documents, airtight, I'll never get to see my daughter again, never see you again," Zach said venomously. "He threatened my life. This was the only way I would get to see you again, Jenna. You have to understand." His voice turned pathetic, wheedling.

"You left our daughter in a parking lot!" she shouted back, rage flowing through her with enough force that she was incapable of thinking logically. She wanted him to drop dead instantly. She didn't care if he took her with him, she wanted to fucking main him in the worst way. He'd caused years of misery with his accusations and legal fights. The final straw was leaving his screaming daughter vulnerable in a parking lot, strapped into her chair. What if the security team didn't find Lola right away? She had to get back to her!

That thought calmed some of her rage. She had to try to reason with him. "Zach, we have to go back! We have to go get Lola. You can't just leave her there for anyone to grab."

She saw the back of his head go side to side in a negative shake. "We can't go back."

"She's our daughter, she could get hurt!" she shouted in disbelief.

"We'll make a new child," he said pleadingly.

She stared at him. Did he actually say that? That they would leave their precious girl behind and go make a new one? Images of his broken bleeding body slashed through her mind giving her small comfort as she worried over what would happen to Lola.

"What's wrong with you?" she cried angrily. "How did you turn into such a monster? I used to love you, Zach. If any part of you still cares for me please, please go back and get Lola."

He seemed to think about it for a second, then shook his head. "We can't. You have to understand, Jenna, if I go back that place is going to be crawling in Corey's guys. He'll take you away, grab me and have me killed. Might even do it himself."

Jenna had never been so angry in her life, not even when Zach was dragging her through the mud, trying to convince the world she was a terrible mother who deserved to lose her daughter. At least back then Lola had been protected, in the care of nannies while Zach tried desperately to keep Jenna in his life. Now, he had what he wanted and it was clear Lola meant nothing to him, dead or alive.

"I want you to die!" Jenna growled, and kicked out with all her might, slamming her feet into the back of his chair. She kept kicking, venting her rage and wriggling closer so she could do some real damage.

"Stop it! Jenna, fuck!" he shouted, trying to shove her flailing legs away.

"No!" She screamed and slammed her feet into the back

of his head sending him flying forward into the steering wheel. He hadn't bothered to put on a seatbelt.

The only warning Jenna had that they were about to crash was the screeching of the tires as Zach hit the brakes. She rolled onto her side and tucked herself against the seats just as they impacted. The air was shoved from her body as her back slammed into the seats with enough force that Jenna lost consciousness for a few seconds.

When she came to, she blinked into the gloom of the back of the van and took a quick inventory of her body. Sore hands from where they were tied behind her back, bump on the head, no broken bones that she could tell. She wriggled her fingers and found the knot on the rope had come loose. It took about a minute of working her fingers against the rough rope before she managed to free herself. She pushed herself onto her knees and looked into the front seat.

Zach was slumped over the steering wheel, unconscious and bleeding from his head. The entire windscreen was smashed, probably from the impact with his head.

"You motherfucker!"

Jenna slammed her fist down onto his shoulder, uncaring that he might have a cracked skull. She was going to finish the job, kill the kidnapping, child abandoning fucker. She smashed her fists into him over and over again, catching him on the face, head and torso, hitting him wherever she could. He didn't move.

The door next to her was jerked open and Jenna let out a yelp of surprise and twisted around to see who was behind her. Vince stood in the doorway, his face a mask of relief, before it melted into something so truly scary even Jenna cringed back. Then she remembered how much he cared about her and Lola. She pointed at her bleeding, broken and unconscious ex-husband and yelled, "He left Lola alone in a parking lot!"

"I have Lola, she's fine," Vince assured her. "She was picked up seconds after he grabbed you. She wants her mama, but otherwise she's unharmed."

"Oh, thank god!" Jenna exclaimed and threw herself at Vince, bursting into tears.

Vince caught her against his chest and held her tightly, pressing his lips to the top of her head as she howled against him. She felt someone touch her back and looked up to find Jared hovering next to them. She gave him a watery smile and reached out to squeeze his hand.

"Take her," Vince said, pushing Jenna into Jared's arms and reaching under his leather jacket.

Jenna gasped when he pulled a gun out and set his knee on the edge of the van. He trained the weapon on Zach's head.

"Stop!" Jenna gasped. "You can't do that!"

Vince twisted around to look at her. "I have to, baby. He's unhinged, he'll just keep coming after you. I refuse to live with his shadow infecting our lives."

"He kidnapped me," Jenna insisted. "He'll go to prison."

"He'll be out in a few years." Vince's voice was flat.

She shook head and reached out for him. Vince ignored her for a second then nodded at Jared who let her go. She took hold of Vince, wrapping her arms around his neck and tugging his face down to hers. "Don't do this," she whispered. "I won't be able to live with myself if you kill him."

"But you'll live, Jenna, and that's all I care about right now. He could've killed you. Worst moment of my life when you I saw you go off the road."

"I'm okay now, I'm not hurt," she assured him, pressing

her lips against his. "He's not worth the stain on your conscience."

Finally, Vince dropped his arm, pulling the gun away from Zach's head. He hugged her tight against his body. "Baby, it's adorable that you think anything could stain my conscience."

"You're not a bad man, Vince."

He snorted, picked her up and carried her away from the scene of the accident. She could hear sirens heading their way.

"Let's go home," she whispered.

"Home," he echoed in agreement and climbed into Jared's truck.

SEVENTEEN

It took some time to calm Lola down, and it broke Vince's heart to see the little girl sobbing in her mother's arms babbling about what'd happened. He wondered how long the trauma would stay with her and vowed to get hold of a child psychologist who could make Lola better. It took hours that night before she was willing to let her mama out of her sight and finally Jenna had to go lay down with Lola in her bed until she fell asleep.

That's where Vince found her, curled onto her side, sound asleep wrapped around her daughter. Lola had her hand tangled in Jenna's hair again and her thumb in her mouth. Jenna had told him that she'd stopped doing that a year ago. It was probably a comforting habit that she needed after such a traumatic day.

Vince bent over and gently untangled the little hand from Jenna's bright red locks, then gathered Jenna into his arms, picking her up. She woke up as he was carrying her down the hall.

"Where're we going?" she mumbled against his shoulder.

"Bed," he grunted.

"Need a shower."

"You can shower tomorrow," he told her.

She yawned widely as he placed her on her feet and shook her head. "I want to wash the smell of this awful day off me. Please, Vince."

It was the please that got him. He couldn't resist when Jenna really wanted something. She'd intrigued him with only a picture, fired his lust at one meeting and stole his heart with those big beautiful eyes, that melodic voice and her precocious daughter. As long as he lived he would never get enough of Jenna. She was it for him, his one and only. When she said please and meant it, he was compelled to listen.

"Okay," he relented. "We shower together then. Don't want you out of my sight."

She smiled sleepily. "I was hoping you'd say that."

Vince stripped her, running his hands over her body as he pulled the clothing away. Each scrape and bruise was another nail in Zach's coffin. The man had hurt Vince's woman and he was going to pay with his suffering before Vince allowed him to go to hell. He had a man keeping an eye on Zach in the hospital, where Zach was recovering from broken ribs, a broken leg and a serious concussion. According to his doctor he would be out of the hospital in a couple of weeks.

Vince stripped himself too and then, taking Jenna's arm so she wouldn't fall, helped her into the shower. She was practically sleeping on her feet. She closed her eyes, leaned against the wall and allowed him to wash every inch of her body, sighing in relief as the heated water passed over her body.

"Lift your foot," he instructed, kneeling to wash her legs

and feet.

She complied and he watched her, thoroughly and with as little lust as he could manage. When he finished washing Jenna he stood and ran the soap over his own body in quick economical movements, wanting to get out of the shower and put Jenna to bed. But before he could turn the water off, Jenna stepped in front of him and wrapped her arms around his neck, tugging his head down to hers.

"Please, Vince, will you... can we...." she stuttered, then blew out a frustrated breath and tried to look him in the eye. "I just want to feel loved. The good kind of love, not the kind that almost got me killed today."

"Oh baby, you are loved, with all my heart and soul. I should've said it so many times by now."

She smiled big and went up on her tiptoes to kiss him, he lowered his head obligingly and gave her as chaste a kiss as he could. The sight and feel of her naked body, her full tits pressing against him was driving him nuts. He needed to get her out of the shower and into some pajamas before he forgot his good intentions and fucked Jenna with a savage need. All of his instincts told him to take her, to touch her, lick her and fuck her everywhere, to affirm to himself that she was unharmed. The tiny ray of chivalry that she'd sparked inside him over the past weeks told him to treat her like she was made out of glass.

As Jenna tried to deepen the kiss, Vince lifted his head and reached for the tap. "No, baby, I don't want to hurt you. Let's go to bed."

She grabbed his wrist before he could shut the water off. She looked him in the eye and said, "I need this, Vince. I need to be reminded that I'm alive and safe, here with you."

Her words echoed his thoughts, still... "We should get out."

"Vince." Her voice took on a stern tone.

"Jenna." His was pleading. "I'm trying to do the decent thing here."

"Vince, fuck me right now." She reached down and wrapped her fingers around his raging hard-on, the one he'd been valiantly attempting to ignore, but that she apparently noticed.

With her words and action that tiny ray of chivalry died. He picked her up and, turning around, shoved her back against the shower wall. She squealed in surprise and then wrapped her arms around his shoulders enthusiastically. He lifted her legs and helped her place them over his hips, bringing her hot little pussy in direct contact with the tip of his cock.

He held eye contact as he slid inside her, pushing until he bottomed out. She moaned loudly and tipped her head back, closing her eyes.

"Look at me," he commanded. "Don't stop."

Her eyes opened, they were glazed with passion and it took her a moment to focus on his face. The second she did, he began moving inside her in slow leisurely strokes. She gasped and moaned as he raked her pussy walls with his cock, over and over. He pressed his hand against her lower back, forcing even more contact between them. With each thrust he grazed her clit and sent her soaring toward the orgasm she was begging for.

Her beautiful blue eyes, locked on him, sent him into a frenzy. He could read every emotion, every bit of pleasure she was experiencing at his hands. It was a powerful feeling, knowing he was the one giving her a release. He began fucking her in long, hard strokes, trying not to press her too hard against the shower wall, but wanting to feel every inch of her, wanting the squeeze of her pussy on his dick as she exploded all around him.

Her nails dug into his shoulder, the sharp bite of pain increasing his frenzy. It was a heady feeling knowing she wanted him as much as he wanted her. That he could take her to paradise and join her there, before they both floated back to reality.

They both orgasmed together, the feeling of her vaginal muscles contracting around him, milking him, drove him over the edge. As she shouted her pleasure, he grunted his release in her ear, while shooting his load of semen deep into her pussy. They stayed connected that way for a few minutes, just holding each other, resting against the wall and breathing deeply.

Finally, Vince gently separated his body from hers, turned the shower off and helped her step out. Her legs wobbled so he made her sit on the edge of the bathtub, which was next to the shower stall, while he dried her off. She sighed happily and closed her eyes, clearly savouring the feeling of him running the towel over her tired body. He realized he probably had minutes if not seconds before she was soundly asleep.

He dried himself quickly and helped her to her feet, guiding her to their bed. He lifted the blankets and she crawled in naked, her head hitting the pillow and a sigh of satisfaction escaping her lips. She was asleep before he even climbed in behind her, wrapping himself protectively around her body. He brushed the hair back from her face, kissed the shell of her ear and whispered, "I love you, Jenna."

He settled down and was about to fall asleep when her sleepy voice drifted through the darkness of the bedroom. "I love you too, Vince."

EIGHTEEN

"Heard you have a date with Sharon," Vince said, lighting up a cigar.

He wasn't a smoker. Not really, but today was a good day for a smoke. It'd been a month since the accident. Jenna and Lola were fully recovered and happily running Vince and his home. He wouldn't want it any other way. His two girls were the world to him, they belonged to him and he planned on taking very good care of them.

"What are you, some kind of gossip now?" Jared grunted his annoyance.

"Hardly," Vince said drily. "Jenna told me this morning before Sharon came over for the day. Apparently they've been planning a spa trip or some shit before the big date."

"Jesus," Jared mumbled. "Was just going to take her out for a drink, maybe dinner at Applebee's or something."

"You need to up your game man. Spa day means you might get some, but not if Applebee's is your date plan."

"I need a smoke," Jared complained, reaching for Vince's cigar.

Vince allowed it, glancing down from where they were

standing. They were on the second level of scaffolding at one of the job sites. Below them was a sea of concrete, slowly filling the pit that would become the parking garage to a brand-new luxury apartment building. It would also become Zach Morris' grave.

Vince watched dispassionately as the broken bleeding man slowly sank into the wet concrete. More concrete was pouring from a truck into the pit. The truck was manned by a guy who knew to look the other way. Vince was satisfied that Zach would no longer present any problems. His disappearance would coincide with a suicide note, outlining his regret over his treatment of his ex-wife. He would also be kind enough to leave his entire estate to his daughter, as was outlined in his new and improved will, signed shortly before his disappearance. Of course, there wouldn't be a body to prove a suicide actually happened, so his estate would likely be tied up for years, but it would be waiting for Lola when she turned eighteen and was old enough to claim her inheritance.

Vince stepped back, slapped Jared on the back and said, "Keep an eye on him, made sure the fuck doesn't manage to crawl out."

Jared snorted. "Would be a little hard with all those broken bones."

Before tossing Zack off the scaffolding into the concrete, they rebroke his freshly healing leg and then went after his other three limbs. Just to make sure he understood he shouldn't try to run away while they administered his punishment. A sound beating followed by suffocating in a bed of freshly poured concrete. Or maybe it was drowning? Vince wasn't sure. He could Google it though, if he really wanted to know.

"Going home?" Jared asked as Vince reached for the ladder.

"Yep, got a date with a hot redheaded."

"Taking her to Applebee's?" Jared teased.

Vince snorted. "Not if I want to get laid tonight. A guy only needs to learn that lesson once."

Jared roared with laughter as Vince climbed down to the ground and strode away. He'd be back in the morning, business as normal. His enemy dead and his family tucked away safely at home. Life didn't get much better than this.

EPILOGUE

"Happy birthday to you, happy birthday to you, happy birthday dear Lola, happy birthday to you!"

Jenna laughter at the godawful singing of a house was filled with guests attending Lola's birthday. She laughed even harder, Vince chuckling at her side, as Lola blew on her candles so hard her little face turned red with the effort. It was her fourth birthday and she was beyond excited for the cake, presents and friends. She bounced around like only a little girl on a massive sugar high could.

"Excuse me," Jenna said, slipping out of Vince's embrace and heading to the kitchen for the plates and forks.

Her mother reached out to squeeze her arm as she passed and Jenna grinned and touched her mom back. It had been a heartbreakingly wonderful reunion when she finally went to see her parents again. They had tearfully accepted her explanation of why she couldn't see them until now, listening to her describe her years with Zach and his constant threats. They were grateful for Vince's presence in her life, he brought Jenna and Lola back to them.

"Hey nurse."

Jenna jumped at the deep voice that interrupted her thoughts as she was reaching into the cupboard for plates.

"How are you Enrico?" she asked carefully.

She was still getting used to his presence. He was released from prison a few weeks ago and Vince had added the big scary tattooed guy to the house security team. At first Jenna had balked, upset that Vince would allow a killer that close to the family. That was the first time Vince told her anything about his past. Though he wasn't explicit in detail, she was left with the impression that Enrico was a fluffy bunny in comparison to Vince. She had finally agreed to have Enrico in her home, though she was still wary. It was one thing knowing that Vince had killed people, but she had experienced Enrico's brutality firsthand when she'd tried to revive a man he stabbed and ultimately killed.

She still didn't understand how he got out of jail so quickly after what happened. Someone, probably Vince, had pulled some strings.

"Let me take those." Enrico lifted the pile of plates and forks from her hands and walked ahead of her back into the living room where the party was being held.

"Oh, thanks," she said, and followed him.

Before she could cross the threshold between the kitchen and the living room, Vince grabbed her around the waist and lifted her right off her feet, carrying her backwards. She laughed and gripped his shoulders, then let out a yelp as he pushed her into the pantry, walked in after her and slammed the door shut.

"Vince - " she gasped, but he cut her off with a kiss that stole her breath and sent her pulse soaring.

In seconds her arms were wrapped around his neck and he was lifting her up, setting her butt on one of the shelves. His hands were everywhere at once, touching her, caressing,

squeezing. Her skin tingled and her belly swirled in anticipation. If she didn't stop him he'd fuck her right there in the
pantry where anyone, including her mother, could walk in.
She tore her lips from his.

"Vince, not here!" she gasped.

"Yes, here," he growled and dragged her head toward his
for another kiss, while he slid a hand under the back of her
shirt and up her body until he reached her bra where he
quickly and skillfully unsnapped it.

"But... people!" she cried.

"I will fuck my wife, when and where I please. Now
stop talking so I can make you come."

Jenna and Vince had gotten married as soon as Vince
could legally get the paperwork and drag her in front of a
Justice. They had now been happily married for seven
months.

He shoved his hand down the front of her leggings and
wiggled them into her panties where he immediately sank a
finger into her wet heat. She moaned her approval and
spread her legs, deciding she would worry about the guests
after her orgasm. Vince was an expert with his fingers,
applying just the right amount of pressure to her clit with
the roughened pads of his fingers. He stopped right before
she could peak and pushed his fingers deep into her pussy,
wiggling them against her g-spot and drawing a gasp from
her. She bit her lip to keep from screaming her pleasure out
loud as he pumped his fingers in and out of her while
pressing the heel of his hand against her clit.

A beautiful, sweet and intense orgasm tore through her.
He swallowed her cries in a kiss and continued to draw her
orgasm out until she had nothing left and lay against the
shelf in a heap.

"My turn," he growled, lifting her off the shelf and

shoving her leggings down. He spun her around until she was facing the shelf.

She could hear him messing around with his belt and zipper. Then he was pressing himself inside her. It was a tight squeeze because he was taking her from behind and there were shelves and stuff in the way. He shifted and something fell off the shelf and hit the floor with a 'poof' sound. Jenna suspected the bag of flour had just been sacrificed in their pursuit of passion.

"Fuck," Vince growled.

Jenna giggled and whispered, "Swear jar."

He took her hair in his fist and forced her to arch back against his chest while he pumped his cock inside her. "Pay attention, baby."

His rough handling heightened her arousal and she had to bite her lip to keep from screaming as his cock raked every pleasure point inside her. The forbidden nature of their little tryst, with Lola's birthday party happening just on the other side of the door, made it even better. Jenna never thought she was into this kind of thing, but since meeting Vince she was becoming more and more eager to share new sexual experiences with him.

"Come with me," he grunted against her ear, biting the lobe.

He reached down her front and fingered her clit, sending her soaring. Seconds later she was desperately trying to muffle her howls of pleasure as he took her over the edge. He followed her over, his cock growing rapidly inside her and then bathing her in semen as he orgasmed. His hands tightened on her body, squeezing her against him as they came down from an incredible high.

"Mommy, daddy, pwesents!" Lola's voice called from the other room.

Vince chuckled, while Jenna scrambled to push him away. She bent down to pull her leggings and panties back up but banged her head on a shelf. "Ouch, fuck!" she exclaimed.

Vince pressed his hand against her forehead and helped her straighten. "Swear jar," he said, humour in his voice. Then he carefully bent down and helped her finish pulling her pants back up.

He zipped and buttoned his jeans and then looked at her, his eyes glowing with love and appreciation. He tucked her hair back behind her ears and bent to kiss her lips then turned to open the door of the pantry. Jenna grabbed his arm to stop him. She took a deep breath.

"Vince, I need to tell you something."

"Yeah, baby, what is it?"

She grinned, beyond happy to share her news. This was one of the best moments of her life and she was about to share it with the man she loved. "I'm pregnant."

His eyes grew round with shock, then he whooped his happiness, picked her up and swung her around, uncaring of the cans and jars that fell to their feet as they knocked things off the shelves. He kissed her heartily and said, "Well let's go tell the birthday girl she's going to be a sister! You heard her, she wants her presents."

THE END

ALSO BY NIKITA SLATER

If you enjoyed this book, check out some other works by #1
International Bestselling Author, Nikita Slater. More titles are
always in progress, so check back often to see what's new!

Angels & Assassins Series

Book One – The Assassin's Wife

The Queens Series

Book One – Scarred Queen

Book Two - Queen's Move

Book Three - Born a Queen (coming 2020)

Alejandro's Prey (a novella)

Fire & Vice Series

Book One – Prisoner of Fortune

Book Two – Fight or Flight

Book Three – King's Command

Book Four – Savage Vendetta

Book Five – Fear in Her Eyes

Book Six – Bound by Blood

Collared: A Dark Captive Romance

Safeword: A Dark Romance

Chained: A Mafia Marriage Romance

Good Girl: A Captive BDSM Romance

Hostile Takeover: An Enemies to Lovers Romance

Visit **nikitaslater.com** for more information
and the latest updates!

STAY CONNECTED WITH NIKITA!

Don't miss one sexy moment. Keep in touch with Nikita for the latest news and updates about all of your favourite characters.

- Check out my **website** for all my book updates!
- Follow me on **Instagram**
- Like and follow me on **Facebook**
- Follow me on **Twitter** (**@NikSlaterWrites**)
- Connect with me on **Goodreads**
- Follow me on **Bookbub**!

Sign up for the newsletter today at receive exclusive updates and access to ***bonus content and chapters*** not available anywhere else!

www.nikitaslater.com
nik@nikitaslater.ca

NIKITA'S UNDERWORLD!

Join Nikita's Underworld, a private Facebook group, for access to exclusive giveaways, WIP, games, book talks and more! Have a burning question to ask Nikita? Drop into Nikita's Underworld!

- **Become part of Nikita's Underworld today!**

ABOUT THE AUTHOR

Nikita Slater is the International Bestselling dark romance author of the Fire & Vice series, Angels & Assassins series, The Queens series and several standalone novels. Her favourite genre is mafia romance, the bloodier the better, though she loves to write about every subject under the sun. She lives on the beautiful Canadian prairies with her son and crazy awesome dog. She has an unholy affinity for books (especially erotic romance), wine, pets and anything chocolate. Despite some of the darker themes in her books (which are pure fun and fantasy), Nikita is a staunch feminist and advocate of equal rights for all races, genders and non-gender specific persons. When she isn't writing, dreaming about writing or talking about writing, she helps others discover a love of reading and writing through literacy and social work.